TOC

TOC

CHAPTER 1 - A Bad Start For John!

It was a Wednesday morning, and John was not having a good day!

He had already missed his usual bus and was now having to walk to work.

Of course it had to be raining as well, and to add to his misery, he managed to get himself well and truly splashed by a car that was driving too fast, through a large dirty puddle.

"At least I've got some sort of job!" He thought. "But what's the use having a Maths and Physics degree, if there are no jobs for Physicists in this rotten town!

I guess I should have looked for a position overseas, like my friend Mark did, instead of just coming back home to Sussex!"
John had finished his degree, at Bristol University, more than six months ago, and had since been forced, to take several minor jobs, back at home, during the past few months.
His present one was as a waiter, in a fast-food restaurant, in the town centre.
Hardly the best use of a four year Msc in Science, to be sure, but at least, it paid the bills.
John, was a well built, six foot, 25 year old, with dark hair and brown eyes.
He was still living with his parents after leaving University, not through choice, but through financial necessity!
But right now, he was wet, dirty and late for work!
"Could it get any worse?" He thought.
He was about to find that it could!!
As he hurried round a corner about 100 yards from his place of work, he failed to notice the hole in the pavement.
His left foot landed in it and he was thrown forward onto his knees before ending up flat on the ground, spreadeagled in a substantial deposit left there by an obviously very large dog.
Getting to his feet he was immediately aware of the odour emanating from most of his clothes.
The smell was hardly likely to be acceptable in his present workplace, or anywhere else, for that matter!
"Is it worth carrying on?" He thought. "Since I can't go into work in this state!"

The obvious answer was of course, No!!
Because there was nowhere to go and clean himself up, he was left with no choice, other than to return home.
Getting a bus or taxi now, seemed equally unacceptable, due to his present state, so he was reduced to having to walk home in the rain.
He therefore turned round, stepped back over the hole, and dashed back round the corner, straight into a woman hurrying towards him.
The collision knocked the woman off her feet, and he landed on top of her.
As he tried to get to his feet once again, he attempted to help her up and apologise for his clumsiness.
The woman looked at him in disgust, as she quickly became aware of the aroma, that she was, by now, sharing with him.
The rain had also became more intense, adding to both his and her misery, for since he had also managed to break her umbrella, she had now lost any protection from the deluge.
John became aware, that her hair was now soaked, and rainwater was dripping down her clothes.
In addition, she had lost one high-heeled shoe, plus the heel of the other, was broken off when John trod on it!
John's situation was getting worse by the minute, and wishing the ground would open up and swallow him, did little good either!
The woman now took a closer look at John.
To say the least, he was not looking great, and of course he didn't exactly smell too sweet, either.

She picked up the remains of her umbrella, and with a swing that a professional golfer would have been proud of, wrapped it round John's neck.
Caught by surprise, John did the decent thing, by collapsing in a heap on the wet pavement!
"That will teach you not to attack an innocent woman in the street!" She shouted. "Scum like you, should be locked up. Were you drunk or on drugs?"
She continued whacking him on the back, as he lay on the ground.
"Help! Help!" She screamed.
A small crowd had gathered around them, despite the rain.
"Get the Police!" The woman shouted. "Before this animal, can get away!"
One of the onlookers, ran off to do as she demanded, while the others stood over John to prevent him getting up.
The rain was still pelting down, harder than ever.
Before long, a Panda car drew up, containing a PC and a WPC, both of whom jumped out, to see what was happening.
The crowd all started talking at once, and the female victim, was still shouting at John, as he lay on the pavement.
Without listening, the constable sized up the situation, and held John down, while his female colleague, handcuffed his hands behind his back!
He was then hauled to his feet and led towards the police car.
"Have you smelled him Frank?" Said the WPC in disgust. "He'll stink our car out!"

"No problem Jan!" He replied. "I'll call for a van to pick him up!"
Five minutes later a police van drew up, and John was pushed roughly into the back, before being driven off!
At the Police Station, two uniformed policemen, marched John inside!
The Sergeant behind the desk, took one smell of John's clothes, and told his constables to take him to a police cell.
Once there, he was given a bowl of water, told to remove his clothes, and put a dressing gown on!
Having done his best to clean himself up, he was visited by a constable, who despite the remaining odour, managed to breathalyse him.
Because the breathalyser proved negative, John was told they were sending for a doctor, to take blood samples to test for drugs!
During all of this time, John tried, over and over, to protest his innocence, but no one took any notice.
Finally a woman doctor arrived, to take his blood sample.
"This is all a mistake!" He said.
"They all say that!" She said without looking at him.
"What were you on this time?"
"Nothing! I don't drink and I have never used drugs!" He said.
"Well we will soon find out, when your samples are analysed!" She said finally.
After she left, someone came in and took his finger prints and a DNA swab from his mouth, before taking him back to the Sergeant at the desk who read him his

rights, and said he would get someone to take down his details.
"We have already, taken a statement from the woman, you assaulted!" Said the Sergeant. "She will be pressing charges so you will probably be appearing in the Magistrates Court, in the morning, if we can arrange it! Until then, you will now be returned to your cell, for the night."
With that, he was returned back to the cell, and provided with a set of overalls.
"This can't be happening!" John thought. "It's all been a terrible mistake!"
He was left alone in the police cell, until lunchtime, when he was provided with a plate of sandwiches, plus a can of Coke.
He sat on the bunk, which was the only furniture in the cell, and ate his sandwiches.
He was not fond of Coke, but he drank half of the can since there was nothing else.
After lunch, he was visited by a young constable who came to take down John's details, on a series of forms.
He told the young P C his name, date of birth, religion etc. and his address.
He also told the constable, that he lived with his parents, and the name and address of his employer.
He was not asked if he wished to make a statement, although he asked to do so.
The rest of the afternoon passed slowly.
John could not tell what time it was, because his watch had been taken away, with the rest of his personal belongings and placed in a sealed bag with a list of contents that he had to sign.

He was told his clothes had been sent to a laundry!
Finally in the evening, he was provided with a hot meal, and a cup of tea.
He was then escorted to the toilet, and wash room, by a pair of constables.
He was given a wash bag containing a flannel, soap, toothbrush and toothpaste, plus a comb, towel and a small aerosol of deodorant (presumably to counteract the smell).
After that he was once again left alone, although from time to time someone came and peered through the small window in the door.
Finally, the main light was switched off to be replaced with a dim nightlight on the ceiling.
John lay down on the bunk and finally managed to fall asleep.
In the morning the main light was switched on again, and John was woken up by a constable.
After once more being escorted to the toilet and Wash room, he was given some cornflakes , toast and tea.
The Sergeant came to see him a short time after his breakfast and told him he would be taken by police van to the Magistrates Court.
A couple of hours later, a constable entered his cell and handcuffed himself to John.
The two of them were then marched out to a waiting police van to be driven the short distance to Magistrates Courthouse.
Once inside, they sat in a room with a couple of other similarly handcuffed couples, before being taken one by one into court.

An elderly man, who he presumed was the Magistrate, was seated behind a large desk, in front of which a man and woman were seated.
John soon realised that the man was the Clerk of Court, and the woman was a Court Secretary.
John was told to stand up, and swear on oath to tell the truth before sitting down again.
He was then ordered, to stand again, while the charge against him was read out.
He was informed that the charges, were being pressed by a Miss Ashmore, who was not present, in court at that time.
But a statement given to the police by her, was read out by the Clerk of Court.
The Magistrate then leaned forward, and addressed John.
"What do you wish to say in your defence?" He asked.
John in reply related politely that what had occurred was an unfortunate accident.
"Do you have any witnesses to corroborate, your version of events?" The Magistrate asked.
"No!" Replied John. "There were only the two of us involved initially. It was all a terrible accident on my part!"
"Miss Ashmore asserted, that you deliberately assaulted her, for no apparent reason, causing her great distress!" Said the Magistrate. "What do you have to say in reply?"
"I can only say that it was an accident. I certainly did not intend to assault her!" Said John.
"Well in the circumstances, I have no option, other than to find you guilty of common assault, upon the

person of Miss Ashmore." The Magistrate stated. "As the Police inform me, you have no previous convictions, I will not impose a custodial sentence in your case. I can however not let your offence go unpunished, so I sentence you to 6 months Community Service plus a fine of 100 pounds! In addition I find you for damages to the person, and property, of Miss Ashmore to the sum of £50. Details of your Community Service will be explained to you in due course by the appropriate agency. You may now leave the Court!"

The policeman released the handcuffs, and escorted John back to the Police van, which returned them to the Police Station.

Once inside,once more, John was given his property back, and his clothes were returned to him laundered and pressed.

The desk Sergeant also handed John a laundry bill of £15 for cleaning his clothes.

John had no option other than handing the Sergeant the money, before he was given a receipt, and allowed to get dressed in his own newly laundered, clothes before leaving.

Outside the Police Station, John breathed a sigh of relief at being free once again!

However, being saddled now with a criminal record, a £150 fine and 6 months Community Service to look forward to, he certainly was not feeling happy.

"All of this, because of a pile of something abandoned by an unknown Canine!" He thought sadly. "And why did Miss whatshername have to be there at that precise moment?"

John walked disconsolately home, only to find that his parents were out.
He felt for his front door key but found it was not in his pocket.
"It must have fallen out when I was on the ground I suppose!" He thought. "So now I can't get in! And I daren't even think of trying to climb in through an open window, if there is one, in case someone sees me and calls the police. I already have a criminal record now, so I could end up back in my cell!"
John's parents had new neighbours on both sides, since he had lived there before going to University, so he didn't see the point of knocking at their doors.
"I suppose I may as well catch a bus into town!" He thought! "At least I still have enough money left, for the bus fare and something to eat! And I guess I had better drop into work as well, to let them know what happened."
He walked disconcernately down to the nearest bus stop, to wait for the next bus into town.

CHAPTER 2 - Another Encounter

"At least it's not raining today!" He thought bitterly.

Someone joined the queue, behind John.

"What times the next bus?" Said the person.

"I don't know!" Said John, turning round.

"Oh no! Not you again!" Said the woman standing there.

John recognised, this was the woman that had caused him all his present troubles.

"I'm afraid so!" Spluttered John, in a bit of a panic. "I will go somewhere else, and get another bus!"

He turned round and started to walk off.

"No wait!" Said the woman, calming down a little. "You don't have to go on my account! Just keep your distance, that's all!"

"I'm sorry for what happened before!" He said apologetically. "It was all my fault!"

"Perhaps it was!" She said quietly. "But maybe I over reacted slightly, as well! You don't seem as bad as you did back then!"

"I'm sorry but I can't engage in small talk, right now!" Said John with a sigh. "You catch the bus! I'll leave you to it!"

John turned and once again,, began to walk back the way he came.

"No wait!" Called the woman. "You're making me feel bad about yesterday."

"Well! Just forget about it Miss Ashmore!" Said John, continuing to walk off.

"How do you know my name?" She demanded, in surprise. "Have you been stalking me or something?"

This was too much for John!

He spun round, and faced her from a distance!

"No! I have most certainly, not been stalking you, or anyone else, for that matter!" He stated strongly.

"So how do you know my name?" She repeated, angrily.

"They told me in Court, of course!" John said quietly.

"Oh! So you have been in Court?" She said calming down slightly. "Because of me I suppose?"

"Why else would I have been there?" John muttered.

"What happened?" She asked with sudden concern.

"It's not your problem!" Said John sharply. "So just forget about it!"

"No! I won't forget about it!" She said more softly. "Please, tell me what happened!"

"I don't want to talk about it now! Thank you!" John replied with a sigh.

"I sense you must have had a bad time, because of me!" She said gently.

"I said I don't want to talk to you about it!" John repeated, heatidly. "So stop asking me about it!"

"Okay! Okay! I will stop mentioning it, if its offending you!" She said soothingly. "But please can't we start this conversation again?" She said carefully. "May I start by introducing myself correctly. My name is Marion Ashmore! Could you, at least tell me your name

"I'm John Taylor!" He stammered, hesitatingly.

"That's a little better, John!" She said quietly. "Do you live here? I have not seen you around recently! Do you live nearby?"

"Yes! I live with my parents, in Prentice Avenue!" John replied, grudgingly.

"Oh! I see! So are you by any chance, Mrs Joan Taylor's son?" She exclaimed.

"Yes!" Said John, reluctantly.

"In that case John! My mum and your Mother went to school together! Haven't you been away at University?"

"Yes I have!" Admitted John.

"Well, I wish we had met under rather better circumstances, John!" She said with a smile. "After our last encounter, I suppose you must hate the sight of me, by now! So i'm sorry!"

John found himself looking at Marion again in a little more detail, since he realised, he could remember little of her, from their previous encounter, yesterday.

Now he saw before him a young women about his age, with light brown hair worn in a ponytail, and a pleasant face with sparkling almond eyes.

He noticed she had quite a slim figure, standing at about six inches less than his height.

"I can understand that you must have similar views, about me now as well!" Said John, dismissively

At that moment, their conversation was interrupted by the arrival of the bus!

"After you!" Said John stepping away politely, to let her board the bus before him.

She stepped onto the bus, and John reluctantly followed her!

"Come and sit with me!" Said Marion taking a seat at the front of the bus,

Since the bus was quite full, and there were no other seats free, John had no option other than accepting her invitation, and sitting beside her!

"Where are you going?" She inquired.

"Only into town!" Said John, dismissively. "Just to have some lunch!"

"It's my day off today, so I'm going to do a bit of shopping." Said Marion, conversationally. "Would you mind if I joined you for lunch, then John?

"I'm only going for a take-away!" Said John, irritably. "I can't afford a decent restaurant at the moment, so, I guess, you would prefer to go somewhere else!"

"Not at all John!" Replied Marion. "I need to watch the pennies too, at the moment!"

"I also, have to call in at the place where I worked as well!" Said John, searching for an excuse. "I need to explain why I did not turn up yesterday, and why I haven't gone in today either, which means I'll most probably get the push anyway, but at least I owe them an explanation, i suppose!"

"You still haven't told me what happened to you yesterday, have you John!" Said Marion again.

"You really don't need to know!" Replied John, beginning to get annoyed.

"Why do you keep saying that?" Persisted Marion.

"Because it's true!" Said John. "So just forget about it! Change the subject! Tell me about you instead!"

"What do you want to know?" Marion asked. "There's not really much to tell! I'm 25 next birthday! I'm single! I work as a Legal Secretary at a Law firm in the High Street! I don't have a car! And I'm getting too old for clubbing now! That's all!"

"I guess that sums me up too at present!" Said John idly. "Having a degree doesn't do me much good right now either! I never imagined that I would end up as a waiter, in a fast-food takeaway joint!"

"Well I'm glad we met today, anyway!" Said Marion. "And i think It's a pity yesterday happened! For my part in it I believe I just over reacted, rather like a silly schoolgirl."

They got off the bus at the terminal, and walked towards the covered shopping mall.

"If you go and make your peace with your boss, John!" Marion said with a smile. "I'll wait for you to join me back here in an hour!f OK?"

Without replying, John walked quickly off to his place of work, and was not surprised to learn, that his services were no longer required.

He was given the wages that he was owed and left.

He had decided, straight away, not to go back to the Mall to meet Marion, so he turned in the opposite direction and walked off!

As he passed a fashion store, his Mother emerged and called to him.

"Where did you get to yesterday, John?" She asked. "Dad and I wondered why you didn't come home last night! Did you stay with one of your University friends?"

"Not exactly!" Said John.

Before he could finish, his mother continued.

"Do you remember my friend, here!" She said, introducing the women standing beside her. "This is Mrs Ashmore John!"

Although surprised by the name, John ignored it, and dutifully shook hands, with his mothers friend.

"Pleased to meet you!" He said, and prepared to leave.

"Nice to meet you as well, John!" Mrs Ashmore replied. "Your mother was just telling me you have done well at University, and I understand you are going to be a Scientist!"

"That's a bit of an exaggeration, I'm afraid!" John replied quickly. "There's not much in the job market, at present!"

Before he could disentangle himself, he heard a voice behind him.

"Ah there you are, John!" Said Marion.

"Oh you've met my daughter!" Said Mrs Ashmore.

"Yes! Mum, he has!" Said Marion, brightly. "Hello Mrs Taylor! We were just off for a bite to eat! See you both, later!"

John was left with no option, except to take his leave from the two women, and follow Marion meekly back to the Mall.

She led him to a cafe, which served tea and sandwiches, just outside the shopping centre.

Escorting him in, they sat down at a table in the corner.

"What do you fancy, John?" Asked Marion, passing John the menu. "I'm paying! I owe you this for the trouble I got you into yesterday! I insist, so please don't argue!"

"I wasn't going to Marion!" Said John reluctantly making his choice. "But yesterday, wasn't your fault, anyway! It was all down to my clumsiness!"

"And my stupid over-reaction, of course!" Apologised Marion gently.

"By the way! How did you get the stench out of your clothes?" Said John changing the subject hurriedly once again.

"I didn't!" She replied, with a grin. "I binned them as soon as I got home! I should think the animal that produced all that could poo for England!"

"Yes! I guess you're right!" Agreed John. "It must have felt a lot lighter after depositing all that!"

"That's better John!" Said Marion with a smile. "At least, you're starting to look a bit more cheerful now!"

"That's because I guess I've hit rock bottom, now!" Replied John, with a shrug. "So i suppose, the only way is up!"

"So are you going to tell me what happened yesterday, John?" She asked again, gently.

"Alright! I give in!" Said John slowly. "I suppose I might as well, if only to stop you mentioning it again!"

He therefore regretfully described, in general terms, the events that he had experienced over the last couple of days!

Marion, was stunned, when she heard about his appearance in Court, and particularly his sentence!

"That's so unfair, John!" She said with concern. "I intend to go to the Court, and inform them that the whole thing was a huge mistake! I'll also take it up with my Law firm!"

"Don't worry about doing that!" Said John bitterly. "It's too late now! And at least I will have a job for a few weeks to keep me amused, even if it's only Community Service!"

"So through me, you lost your job as, well!" Said Marion, feeling devastated.

"Yes! But it certainly wasn't the most exciting, job in the world, anyway!" John replied finally,

"All because of my stupidity, though!" Repeated Marion with a frown.

"No! Because of my clumsiness, as I've said before!" Replied John, insistently

"Now don't go getting all gloomy again, John!" Said Marion, feelingly. "I prefer you, when you're more upbeat, even if you don't have much to be cheerful about, at the moment!"

"Oh I'll, survive!" Declared John, with a shrug. "If I don't get beaten up by your boyfriend!"

"What makes you think I have a boyfriend?" Demanded Marion with a frown.

"I just assumed you would be surrounded with, admirers!" Said John, apologetically

"Well I'm not!" Said Marion firmly. "As I told you before, I'm single! And I intend to stay that way unless the right person comes along!"

"Sorry Marion!" Said John. "That's none of my business! Perhaps I had better be going, before i comit any more *'faux pas'*, and just leave you to let you get on with your shopping!"

"Oh so you want to get rid of me, now?" Smiled Marion grimly. "I guess I do go over the top a bit, don't I?"

John slowly began to realise that he didn't actually totally dislike, this young woman, who had caused him so much trouble a couple of days ago, but he thought it was about time, that he walked out of her life, and stopped causing her any more, grief!

"I had better go, now Marion!" Said John hurriedly. "I need to get back to my parents, to spend, at least one, day at home. Thanks for the sandwiches though! See you!"

John got up swiftly, and left the Café.

"I don't usually, have that kind of effect on people!" Thought Marion, sitting alone, sadly. "I was really beginning to like, John, but I guess our encounter yesterday, must have been the last straw, as far as he was concerned!"

She stood up, feeling unhappy as she watched him leave, paid the bill, and walked away!

John, meanwhile, made his way home to find his father, Richard, had returned from work, and was waiting for his mother, to return from her shopping outing.

"Hi stranger!" His father said, brightly. "Where did you get to yesterday? Did you meet one of your ex-Uni friends?"

"No Dad!" Replied John. "I had a bit of a bad day, yesterday!"

"How do you mean?" Said his father with concern. "You're not ill are you?"

"Nothing like that Dad!" Said John.

He related the events of the last 36 hours, yet again, without mentioning Marion's involvement!

When he told his father about his Court appearance, and his Sentence, his parent was horrified.

"Does your mother know about this, John?" Asked his father.

"Not yet Dad!" Replied John. "But she soon will I'm afraid, because I saw her down the town, with Mrs Ashmore."

"What has Sue Ashmore, got to do, with your mother knowing what happened, to you?" Said his father.

"Because it just happened to be her Daughter, that I bumped into, that started all that followed!" Explained John. "I was accused of assaulting her!"

"Well I will have to go and get her, to retract her statement!" Said his father, angrily. "If, as you say it was an accident! I never did like the stupid girl!"

"No Dad!" Said John quickly. "I have already met her, and apologised. She, in turn, is now sorry, for over reacting on the spur of the moment!"

"That's all very well, from her point of view!" Said his father. "Because she hasn't got a criminal record now, has she, John?"

"No she hasn't dad!" Agreed John with a sigh. "But, at least, she told me that she feels bad about the way things turned out, anyway!"

"As well she, should, of course!" Said his father, vehemently. "I dread to think, what your Mother will think, when she gets home, John! Oh and by the way, you have a letter waiting for you! Looks like a Council one!"

John opened the letter, which informed him, that he was required to report to one of the Council Offices, on Monday, in a week's time, at 8 o'clock in the morning.

He wondered what delights awaited him on Monday week, and decided it would not be a good idea to be late.

His father, was not overjoyed, to think his son, was going to spend the next 6 months, in the company of, what he regarded as a 'bunch of yobbo's'.

When John's mother returned half an hour later, she was also not very happy, having heard from her friend Mrs Ashmore's Daughter, what had occurred.

Although Marion had tried to soften the blow, saying that it was all a misunderstanding, and John should not have been convicted, the two ladies would not accept her insistence that he was not guilty.

"What's the matter with you John?" His mother shouted, angrily. "You've brought disgrace on our family! What will the neighbours say when they find out!"

"I've already had that conversation with him Joan!" Said Richard, soothingly "We will just have to live with it!"

"It's alright for you Richard!" Said Joan bitterly. "You are out at work all day! I have to meet people round here every day, including the neighbors as well as Sue Ashmore!"

John began to fee rather like a naughty schoolboy, after his parents comments.

"I'm sorry it upsets you both!" Said John. "But I am not too chuffed with the idea either!"

Little more was said while they sat down for their evening meal, although the atmosphere was decidedly frosty!

After the meal John diplomatically decided it was time to go to bed, ready for an early start in whatever the morning.was likely throw up.

The atmosphere over the next few days remained less than exciting from John's perspective!

He decided to spend the weekend safely indoors, reading one of his books, rather than risk meeting the dreaded Marion, or, even worse, one of her parents!

Inevitably, a week later, Monday morning arrived!

CHAPTER 3 - Community Service.

John woke early on the Monday morning, in question, and after a quick breakfast he said farewell to his parents and set off for the relevant, Council Office.
He was greeted, by a middle aged man, in a Hi-Viz yellow jacket.
The man introduced himself, as Mr Harris, an ex Police Constable, who was now in charge of work allocation, for offenders undergoing, Community Service.
John was issued with an orange pair of overalls, plus a Hi-Viz Jacket, similar to that worn by Mr Harris.
He was shown into a room containing a number of metal lockers!
John was allocated one which Mr Harris unlocked!
"You may place any of your personal effects in this locker!" Said Mr Harris. "Offenders are not permitted to have mobile phones, watches, any formed of jewellery, cigarettes or tobacco, during their duty hours. The key will be returned to me once you have put on your overall and your Hi-Viz jacket. I see you are wearing trainers, which is fine, but boots are available if you wish to use them. Remember alcohol and tobacco products are not permitted during your working hours. New overalls will be issued once a fortnight and any other safety items such as gloves, headwear etc. will be issued as required."
"Today, you will be part of a team, engaged in the removal of graffiti. The tools that you will be using, will be in the council lorry, that will take you to the

areas, where you will obe working. You will be supervised by Mr Sanjit, who will also be driving the lorry. Your team will number 10 persons, including yourself. So Let's go and meet your team mates."
John was led outside, into a yard, with a number of people, all suitably attired, seated on benches, next to a council Transit van.
Mr Sanjit was introduced to John, by Mr Harris.
The members of the 'team' were not introduced, to John so they were left to do their own introductions, if they required to do so!
They were a mixed bunch of men, mostly younger than John, from a variety of ethnic, backgrounds.
As he had been told, they were all wearing the same outfits, as indeed, was Mr Sanjit.
Without further ado, they were all told to climb aboard the Transit van, by Mr Sanjit, and they set off.
John found himself, sitting on a seat in the van, next to a young West Indian lad, aged about 18 or 19.
"Hi I'm Josh!" He said with a smile. "This your first time? What are you called?"
"John!" Replied John. "And yes, it is indeed, my first time!"
"Is that your real name, or just a nickname?" Said Josh.
"My real name!" Said John. "Why shouldn't it, be?"
"Oh, it's just that some of us, don't like using our real names, while we're here, in case rival Gang members, will then know how to target us or our mates!" Said Josh. "My big brother, Nat, got shot last year, by a rival gang."
"That's bad!" Said John.

"Not so!" Laughed Josh. "He wasn't killed, anyway, he was only nicked! So he had the guy that shot him, worked over by his buddies! His street cred, went through the roof!"
"Don't take too much notice of, Josh!" Said a white skinhead, sitting opposite John. " He fantasises, all the time!".
"I do not!" Denied Josh. "You know nothing, Bulldog!"
"Shut up you, two!" Retorted an Indian or Pakistani, man about Johns age. "Sanjit will report you to Harris, if you're not careful!"
"You shut up Poppadom!" Said Bulldog, belligerently. "Who pulled your chain?"
"Shut up back, there!" Shouted Mr Sanjit from the driver's seat.
The rest of the journey passed quietly, without incident, and they arrived at a place, near the railway station, with a long tall wall covered by various messages and drawings sprayed on it in various, colours.
They were all told, to climb off the Transit van, by Mr Sanjit, and get the required items, needed to clean the wall, which was about 30 feet, long.
They were split into teams of 3 or 4, and spread out along the wall.
They all got to work, with cleaning materials, plus brushes and scrapers, to remove as much of the 'artwork' as, possible.
Strangely enough, they all seemed quite happy, in their duties, which surprised, John.

He found he was working with Josh and Bulldog, and was rather surprised to discover that they both seemed to get along happily, with one another, despite their earlier, arguments.
Josh especially, always seemed cheerful, and seemed to have a permanent grin, on his face.
The morning passed quickly, and soon Mr Sanjit announced, that it was time for a break for lunch!
Lunch boxes were taken out of the van, and handed to everyone.
John opened his, to find two packs of sandwiches, a can of orange Tango, an apple, and a packet of crisps.
He found, each lunch box, had different contents, and people began to swap items, with each other.
John swapped his cheese sandwiches, for ham and egg ones, with Poppadom, and his apple, for a banana, with a West Indian chap, called Ratbag.
They either sat in the Transit van, or on the ground beside it!
They were reminded by Mr Sanjit, that no one was allowed to smoke, or have cigarettes!
This did not bother John, since he had never smoked, but some of his companions, moaned.
The chap they called Poppadom, came and sat with John, Josh and Bulldog.
"How did you end up, here?" He asked John.
John explained what had happened to him, and why he was in his present situation.
"So like most of us, you weren't guilty, either!" Said Josh, swiftly. "I 'spose you cum up, b'for old smart-arse Baker, then!"

"That's why you got a, sixer" Said Poppadom. "Sted of a three-er, which is the most you should have got, for that"
"Pity old Missies Barnes, wasn't on for, you!" Chimed in Bulldog. "You might have got off, with a slap on the, wrist!"
"Yeah!" Said another West Indian youngster, called Bigshot. "My bro got off when she was, on. He said he woz being bullied, when he shot Oddpot in the leg, and she believed him!"
Mr Sanjit told them to stop showing off, in front of their new workmate.
After an hour lunch break, they were required, to carry on with their, work until, about 5 o'clock, when they were told, to load their cleaning materials, back on the Transit, before Mr Sanjit, took them back to the Council yard.
They were all required to sign an attendance book, before leaving to return to their homes, or lodgings for the night.
John handed back his Hi-Vis jacket, but was told to keep his overall, which he wore home.
Josh reminded him, they issued new ones every, two weeks.
John returned home, to find his parents still upset, but at least now resigned, about his Community Service.
His mother decided to wash John's overall , saying she did not wish the neighbours, to see her son, going out in dirty, clothes!
The following day, John was informed that the routine, would be the same, at various locations, around the town, for the rest of the week!

On Friday, he found they were paid a basic ' wage', which was laid down by the Local Government, guidelines.
He also found the weekends, were non-working days, so John was able to relax.
He decided to stay at home again, rather than go out!
He sometimes wondered, how Marion was getting on, but decided on reflection, it was probably sensible, not to attempt, to see anything of her.
On Monday, the work routine, commenced again.
John was pleased to find, that he was working with most of the same group of people, apart from a couple of men that had finished their sentences, and been signed off, plus one or two newcomers.
Josh, Bulldog and Poppadom, took a liking to John, for some reason and they all became quite, friendly.
John learned that Josh, had been in trouble with the police, since he was 10, and had received a number of ASBO's, over the years.
His present Community Service, was imposed after he was arrested, for being caught breaking and entering, by the police.
Bulldog, said he was arrested, for beating up a man from a rival gang, with a baseball bat.
He said, he got a nine month sentence, and he still had nearly 6 months, to go.
Poppadom, who announced he was married, it turned out, had been found guilty, of beating up a white neighbour, who had called him a dirty, black Wog!
He only had 3 more weeks, to go!
Josh told John he now wanted to 'go straight', and get a proper job, when his time was up!

Bulldog, said he wanted to go back sometime, to where he used to live, but wouldn't say where that, was!
Another week went by, followed by another.
Poppadom, finished his time, and said a final farewell, to John, and his companions!
John was surprised, that no new people, joined his 'team' - Mr Sanjit informed them, the 'Graffiti Squad', as he referred to his 'workers', must be doing a good job, because new offenders, were being allocated to different, duties.
John's group, moved to several different locations, around the town, and their 'remit' changed from removal, to covering, up - meaning they used paint, to hide the efforts, of some of the 'artists' creations, which were difficult to remove!
Josh, in particular, began to enjoy his new role as painter, and took great pride, in producing a good 'finish' to his work!
"Perhaps I could get a job, as a Painter when I finish, here!" He said happily, one day.
Bulldog and John were less impressed, with the change in their 'duties' since they both, tended to get more paint on themselves, than they put on the walls.
Despite this, John settled into a routine, and found the time passed quite quickly, in fact he got rather annoyed on a couple of occasions, when rain meant they couldn't work.
Soon, he found he had completed his first month, of his sentence.
Only 5 more to go!

He now, although he no longer resented his sentence, and despite making no attempt to see her, he had not forgotten about Marion.
His mother, told him that Mrs Ashmore, had informed her, that Marion had been to the Court, and also the Police, and retracted her statement, that had convicted John.
As expected, nothing had come of her attempts.
John lost interest, when his father kept saying, that he was determined, to see the family name, cleared and John, pardoned.
As far as John was concerned, he was doing his time, and maybe even performing a useful service, for the neighbourhood.'
Mr Sanjit's team moved on to other tasks, after another month went by!
They were involved in various tasks, such as litter removal, weed removal, fence repairs and even, on occasion, gardening!
Bulldog, Josh and John, continued to co-operate, with Mr Sanjit's approval, as one of his best 'teams', on the various tasks, assigned to his, 'group.
And so life, continued for John, until one Monday, when Mr Harris announced, that this was his last week.
John almost, but not quite, felt sorry that his sentence, was coming to an end.
It meant, he was going to be saying goodbye, to his newfound friends, and it also meant, he would have to find himself, some sort of job, once again.
Finally Friday, came!

Mr Sanjit bade him a fond farewell, and Mr Harris, then signed him off for the last, time.
By now, it was the late autumn and every day, it was getting dark, when he finished his work, each evening! As he walked home, in the darkness, without his orange overalls, which he had to return, he found Josh, walking beside him.
"I've got another two weeks, to do!" Said Josh. "Do you think, I will ever get a job, John? I don't think there's much I can do, really, cause I never spent much time at, school. Would you show me how to read and write, sometime. Cause I never learned that, proper! I know, I would need to read and write, to apply for a job, wouldn't I? I would pay you for it, of course! I saved up all the money they gave me, here."
"I will teach you for nothing, Josh!" Said John. "You have been a good mate, to me for the last 6 months, and so has Bulldog - I never did find out how he got that name."
He gave Josh his parents phone number and asked him to him to ring, when his Community Service, finished!
"Thanks a lot, John!" Said Josh as he walked off, to wherever he was living.
It seemed almost strange, to have completed his sentence, and he began to think, about what the future would mean for him, now he had a criminal record, to contend with!
"I don't think my Uni degree, will be much use, now!" He though bitterly. "I guess I will have to aim a bit lower, now! Perhaps I could do a bit of private tutoring, if guys like Josh, need a bit of help!"

He strolled along, in the dim light, from the few street lights, that were still working - the side streets, on his way home, were never brightly, lit!
As John neared his parents house, he was surprised, to hear someone calling his, name.
"Hello John!" He heard.
"Who's that!" He said, mystified.
"It's me!" Said Marion, coming up behind him, into the nearest streetlight, out of the darkness.
"Oh hello!" Said John with surprise. "What can I do for you?"
"Just speak to me!" Marion replied quietly. "I know you have been avoiding me, John! But I have been missing seeing, you!"
"I'm afraid I have been a bit busy, lately!" Said John bitterly. "If you remember!"
"I know!" Said Marion with a sob. "I still feel wretched, about what happened to you, and it's all my fault! My mum, says your mum does not want to talk to her now, all because of me! I wish I could do something, to make things right between them! They've been friends since school!"
"I expect you must wish, you had never met me as well, Marion! Don't you?" Said John.
He regretted the remark as soon as he said it.
He thought to himself "Marion did not deserve, that!"
"I'm sorry I disturbed you, John!" She said softly.
"Please forgive, me! I'll go!"
She turned away, and began to walk off.
"Wait!" Said John gently, feeling, wretched. "Please come back!"

Marion took a step back towards John, with her eyes on the ground.
John held out his hand.
"I'm so sorry, Marion!" He said holding her hand. "That was unkind of, me! I didn't realise how much I've really missed seeing people lately, while I have been paying my debt to, society!"
"Thank you John!" She said quietly. "Could we possibly start again please!"
John, reached over and wiped away a tear that was dropping off the tip of her nose.
"That's better Marion!" He smiled. "It's a shame to spoil such a nice face!"
"Oh John! I thought I had lost you, forever!" She said shyly. "I was sure you never wanted to see me again! I realise I'm being a silly schoolgirl again! If you would let me, I would like us to be friends! Ill try not to be a nuisance to you! I promise!"
"I don't want you to change!" Said John calmly "I'd like you to stay, just the way you are!"
"So can we be friends again John?" Asked Marion quietly. "I do need a friend at the moment! Don't worry! I'm not expecting you to want to be my boyfriend or anything like that! Just a friend would be nice!"
"Why wouldn't I, or anyone else, want to be your boyfriend, Marion?" Said John gently squeezing her hand. "Anyone would be honoured to have the pleasure of that! Maybe even a stupid idiot, such as me!"
"Do you mean that John!" Marion said softly. "Or are you just humouring me!"

"Of course I do!" Replied John with a smile. "And I promise I will keep well away from dog droppings from now on!"
"You shouldn't say that!" She smiled."Because that unknown canine brought us together. Without him or her, we might never have met!"
"Okay I'll drink to him or her for that!" Said John, getting bored "Now I will have to let you go, I'm afraid! It's probably not a good idea for you to be seen with me right now! I'm still a 'criminal' you know! But please can I ask to see you tomorrow Marion! Because I would very much like then, to continue this conversation!"
"Oh yes please! So would I John!" She replied, suddenly looking happier. "Could we maybe meet in the cafe in town where we last ate together?"
"That would be really nice!" Said John gently, feeling generous. "I'll see you there at about 12 o'clock if you can get time off work, and that's not too early! And this time it will be my turn to pay! Okay?"
"No! That's fine!" She said. "That's my lunch hour! I can hardly wait!"
Marion gave John a quick kiss on the cheek and hurried off smiling happily.
John continued to his parents house also in a slightly more contented mood, Even, sort of, looking forward, to their intended meeting, tomorrow!

CHAPTER 4 - Next Day Brings a Surprise

John woke up early next morning and after a wash and shave, ate his breakfast, and despite his apprehension, the still left to catch the bus at 11 o'clock into town to meet Marion.

He found the bus was late arriving at his stop and was further delayed due to heavy traffic going into town.

The result was John found himself half an hour late when he finally arrived at the cafe where he had arranged to meet Marion.

"She'll think I'm not coming!" He thought. "Or maybe that I've chickened out again!"

He walked into the cafe and went over to the table that they sat at when they were there before.

There was still no sign of Marion.

He sat down and the waitress came over to take his order.

"I was waiting for a young lady!" Said John looking around. "I don't suppose you would know if she's been in!"

"No one has been in for the last hour!" The waitress replied. "Can I get you something while you are waiting!"

"Yes I'll have Cup of hot chocolate please" Said John.

An hour went by with no sign of Marion.

"Looks like I've been stood up!" Thought John bitterly."Is she trying to teach me a lesson or something, by making a fool of me!"

He waited another half an hour before giving up.

He paid his bill, left and walked aimlessly around the Mall for about an hour before calling it a day, and heading for the bus to go home.

When he got home his parents were out - his father was at work and he knew his mother was going to the hair salon.

He made himself some lunch and settled down with a book to pass the time.

His mother returned at about 4 o'clock in the afternoon.

"I thought you were out for the day John!" Said his mother. "Have you been looking for a job?"

"No Mum!" Said John. "I went to meet someone but they didn't turn up!"

"Anyone special John?" She asked.

"No!" Replied John. "Just one of the guys I was working with for the last 6 months."

"Never mind!" Said his mother. "Some people can't be relied on these days!"

A couple of hours later Johns father came in from work.

"I've Just bumped into David Ashmore Joan!" Said John's father to his mother. "It seems his daughter did not come home last night, and there's no sign of her tonight either!"

"Are you talking about Marion Ashmore?" Asked John.

"I guess so!" Said his Mother. "They have only one daughter. Their other child is a son. Of course you knew who she is John didn't you? She was the one that got you arrested 6 months ago, wasn't she?"

"Yes she was!" Replied John beginning to feel worried.

Nothing more was said and John began to feel more and more apprehensive.

"Why would she go off like that!" He thought. "She seemed fine last night. Even happy. Was that all an act for my benefit perhaps!"

No he decided quickly.

He did not believe she could be as mean as that.

Surely she couldn't have had an accident last night, because she was only a few steps away from her house.

If she had fallen down or something surely he would have heard or seen her!

He went to bed eventually still feeling uneasy.

The following morning when John went downstairs he was greeted by his mother.

"I've just been speaking on the phone to Mrs Ashmore!" Said his mother. "She said Marion did not come home again last night. She rang the firm where her daughter worked and they told her Marion hadn't been there for the last two days! As a result, Mr Ashmore has now rung the police and reported her missing. The Police are sending someone round to take their details this morning. I hope for the Ashmores sakes Marion is soon found."

John now began to get really bothered.

What could have happened to her?

Why had she gone away?

Was it something he had said or done last night?

Surely she couldn't have gone off with a friend or something.

Or worse still could she have been kidnapped or attacked by some weirdo?

John became more and more agitated and began to feel helpless.

The morning dragged by and Marion's disappearance made John even more worried.

At 1o'clock a police detective knocked on their door.

"I am making routine inquiries about a missing person from the next street!" He said. "Mrs Ashmore told me you were a friend of hers, Mrs Taylor! Could you tell me the last time you saw her daughter Marion."

"I saw her about a fortnight ago when I went round for coffee with Mrs Ashmore." Replied John's mother."Marion was off work with a cold at the time or something!"

"What about you?" The Detective said turning to John. "I gather she was the person that had you arrested and charged with assault. Can you tell me when you last saw Miss Ashmore!"

"I think it was about 6 months ago!" Said John quickly. "I expect you know where I have been for that time!"

"Yes!" Said the Detective. "You have been serving a sentence bought about this time by your assault on Miss Ashmore. Did it make you resentful about her causing you the inconvenience?"

"No it did not!" Replied John forcefully.

"Thank you both for your time." Said the Detective. "If you have any knowledge or reason why Miss Ashmore should have left home, please contact me or ring the Police Station!"

When the policeman left, John's mother was worried about the detective talking about John's involvement with Marion.

"It seems as if they were looking at you as a suspect for causing Marion's disappearance!" She said.

"I don't know why!" Said John quickly. "Just because I bumped into her 6 months ago!"

"Well they always seem to go for the easiest option I believe!" Said his mother.

"Well I've done my time now!" Said John wearily. "So they will have to find someone else on this occasion! Won't they Mum?"

John spent the rest of the day worrying about Marion!

Had she gone off somewhere, or had someone taken her away?

Who could have taken her and why?

Where were they keeping her?

Was she even still alive?

"If only I could help in some way!" He thought. "But, since no one knew that we met the night that she disappeared, if I admit that we did, I will probably be arrested for questioning and locked up again! Because they didn't believe me last time, why would they believe me now?"

John was in a quandary!

He felt desperate to do something to try and find her or to help someone else to do so.

He did not know what to do!

He could not even think of anyone that he could turn to for assistance!

By the evening he heard that the Ashmores had received a ransom note from whoever was holding Marion.

No one disclosed the amount of money being requested or any other information although the police must have known about it.

Of course John could hardly go and see the Ashmores and ask them for details, because as far as they were concerned, Marion and himself were not even on friendly terms!

Another three days passed with still no news about Marion.

John was becoming more and more worried and could still do nothing to help the search for her.

There was still no one that he could turn to for advice or help!

His parents were no more helpful either for the same reason.

His father even said it served her right, because of all the trouble that she had caused to John and his family!

At about 9 o'clock in the evening on the next day the phone rang.

John went and answered it.

"That you Taylor?" Said a man's voice.

"I think you want my mother or father?" Said John. "Hang on I'll get them!"

"No it's you I want John Taylor!" The voice said quickly. "I saw you with your girl friend,, the other night! If you ever want to see her again, you will go to Blake's Mill, tomorrow at 11 o'clock! Tell no one and come alone! Or else!"

Before John could say anything, the phone went dead.

"Who was that on the phone?" Called his mother.

"Wrong number!" Said John quickly.

John was even more uncertain what to do now.

"Me and Marion are hardly a couple!" Thought John. "We scarcely know each other really! But it looks like the idiot who just rang, thinks I fancy her. What do I do now? Should I do the right thing and ring the Police? If not, why should I go to wherever Blake's Mill is! I'm hardly the right person anyway! Am I? Shouldn't that call

The voice had told him to tell no one and come alone.

He knew in these cases the police should be informed, but he didn't want to go to them for obvious reasons.

And he also didn't want to confide in his parents, for the same reason.

The phone rang again John grabbed the receiver quickly.

"Hello!" He said roughly.

"Hello John! It's me Josh!" Said his ex Community Service friend. "Are you still able to teach me to read and write. If not I won't bother you!"

"Of course I will Josh!" Said John, kindly. "When do you want to start?"

"Next Monday if that's alright." Said Josh. "I've just finished my sentence!"

"No problem!" Replied John. "While you're on the phone Josh. Can you tell me where Blake's Mill is?"

"You mean the old Watermill down by the river on Jarvis Avenue." Said Josh. "Why do you want to go there? It's deserted now, but Bulldogs old mates used to meet there a few months ago I believe. I don't think they have used it since Bulldogs not been around. Why did you ask?"

"Oh! Someone I know, wanted to know about it!" Said John. "Never mind! It's not important! I'll see you on Monday Josh! Goodbye!"

John could not remember where Jarvis Avenue was, so he went to get the local map from the lounge.

"Why am I even bothering!" He wondered.

His mother came in before he found it.

"Who was the second call from?" She asked.

"It was from Josh, a chap I met when I was doing my Community Service!" Said John. "He wants me to teach him, how to read and write!"

"That's good of you John." Said his mother. "Where does he live?"

"I think he said Jarvis Avenue!" Said John, thinking quickly. "I don't know where that is. So I said I would teach him here!"

"Jarvis Avenue is down by the river." Said his mother. "It's become a bit of a rough area now, but it used to be quite upmarket about 20 or 30 years ago! I remember, there's used to be an old watermill down there once. If it's still there now it must be deserted by now. Anyway I'll show you where Jarvis Avenue, is on the map."

She got out the local map and pointed out where the old watermill used to be situated, in Jarvis Avenue.

John thanked her, saying he would not need to be going there anyway, now that Josh was coming here to their house.

John said goodnight to his mother and went to his room to sleep.

"The person on the phone had not asked him to bring any money!" Thought John. "That's a bit odd! That isn't the way the Ransom business is supposed to work! Is it? So why does want me to go there? Has he muddled me up with someone else? But he reckons he saw me on that night with Marion! Strange!"

John began to get, more and more confused! "Why had he been asked to go there! He thought. "Rather than someone from Marion's family? Was someone trying to kidnap him, as well?"

The whole business seemed to be getting weirder and weirder!

Finally, curiosity got the better of him, so he became determined, to go to Blake's Mill tomorrow as he was directed, just to see what happened!

CHAPTER 5 - Blake's Mill

Next morning, John told his parents, that he had decided to go out job hunting.

He took the bus into town, before making his way to Jarvis Avenue.

Once he arrived, he discovered Jarvis Avenue, was a long winding tree lined road, about a mile and a half in length.

He noticed at the top end, there were a few large 4 or 5 bedroom detached houses on both sides of the road, and the last one was about half a mile from where he was standing!

Further down, there was a block of 8, run-down deserted terraced houses, on the left side of the road, with open countryside on the other. Beyond that, there were no other buildings for about three quarters of a mile, leaving only a rather overgrown countryside, with just a few scattered trees, dotted about.

Finally, in the distance, John could just see what looked like a river, through some larger trees.

Setting off, he walked steadily down the long road, until finally, rounding the last bend, he could see it was a river in front of him! and a building

On the left side was a building of some sort, standing about 60 or 70 yards back from the road.

He could see that the building looked deserted, and run down, among the few weeds and shrubs that surrounded it, whilst opposite, on the other side of the road,

there was a small wood with a number of tall pine trees.

John looked across at the building, and quickly noticed that it had a faded sign on the wall, identifying it as Blake's Mill.
While, deciding what to do next, he spotted a figure emerging from the trees, a little further down towards the river.
John recognised the man straight away.

"Hello Bulldog!" He said with a surprise.

"Hello yourself, John!" Said Bulldog walking up to him. "What on earth are you doing here?"

"I was about to ask you, the same question!" Laughed John.

"I often used to come here fishing!" Said Bulldog holding up a bag with a fishing rod. "But as you know, I've been otherwise engaged for a while, so this is the first time I've had a chance to come down again, until now! It should still be a good place for pike if you know where to look! Not many people come down here now though. You interested in fishing John? If so, I'll show you the best places!"
Before he could answer, the sound of a shot, came from the direction of the old Mill, and Bulldog collapsed on the ground.
John, instinctively dropped beside him, and as another shot rang out, grabbed Bulldog by the arm, and pulled him back, towards the trees behind him.
Two further shots rang out, without luckily, finding either of human targets, who were, by now, partly hidden, by a few small bushes, plus a slight rise in the ground.

John was aware of the bullets hitting the trees behind him, but he continued to pull the obviously injured, Bulldog, back under the cover of the trees.
Although he could not hear the sound of any more shots, coming from the Mill, he became worried, in case, whoever was doing the shooting, might come after them!
He listened for any sounds of movement, as he knelt beside Bulldog, who was swearing quietly, and obviously in pain.
"I'm sorry for pulling you about, like this!" Said John gently. "Does it hurt? Where were you hit?"
"Yes! I'm afraid it bloody well does!" Groaned Bulldog, wincing with pain. "It's my damned right shoulder, and I can't move my arm!"
"Just lie still for a moment!" Whispered John. "I think, I'll have to get your jacket off, so I can have a look at your shoulder! I'm afraid it could hurt a bit! Are you ready?"
He gently began to help Bulldog, who groaned in pain, as John slowly managed to remove his leather jacket.
He could see, at once, that there was blood, on both the front and back of Bulldog's t-shirt.
Bulldog groaned once more, and muttered a few more choice swear words.
"I'm afraid I need to get your shirt off, as well Bulldog!" John said. "So that I can stop the bleeding! I'll try to be as carefully as possible!"
"Don't worry about that, John!" Gasped Bulldog with a groan. "Just get the ruddy thing off!"
John gently helped Bulldog to remove his t-shirt and helped him to sit up!

He used Bulldog's t-shirt, to wipe away some of the blood on his chest and back.
John could now see, that the bullet had passed straight through his shoulder, and saw that there was surprisingly, very little blood, oozing from the wounds at his chest or back.
John removed his own t-shirt, and tore both of them into strips, which he used to form a makeshift bandage of sorts, for Bulldogs shoulder, as well as he could.
He was still concerned about the person who fired the shots, so leaving Bulldog propped against a tree trunk, he carefully looked round for a place, which would allow him to see across, towards the old Mill, without being seen.
He could see no signs of movement from the building, but suddenly a motorbike came racing along the road, from the direction of the river, before speeding away up Jarvis Avenue.
John saw that It was driven, by a person dressed all in black leather, wearing a black crash helmet.
He also noticed that there was a long package strapped across the rider's back, which John assumed, could possibly contain a rifle of some sort.
Anyway, the motor cycle and its passenger sped away, and disappeared up Jarvis Avenue.
John went back to Bulldog who had, by now, managed to climb unsteadily to his feet, and was leaning with difficulty, shakily onto a tree trunk.
John told Bulldog, what he had witnessed, before telling him that they would need to try to make their way, slowly back up Jarvis Avenue in order to get him to safety.

Bulldog said he was able to walk, but understood, that the journey back was going to be a bit painful, for him!
John put Bulldogs left arm through the left sleeve, of his leather jacket, and wrapped the rest of the jacket, carefully over his injured right shoulder! He also managed to fasten the lower part of the zip, to try to hold the jacket in place.
Bulldog put his left arm around Johns shoulder, and they made their way, slowly up Jarvis Avenue!
The journey, with several stops, for Bulldog to rest, took nearly an hour! Although John tried several of the houses, at the top of the road, he found that they were either deserted, or at any rate, no one bothered to answer, so they were forced, to carry on slowly towards town.
Eventually they managed to reach the outskirts of town, where John managed to find someone to phone for an ambulance, to take Bulldog and himself to the hospital.
Once there, John told the doctor that examined Bulldog, that someone down by the river had shot him. One of the hospital staff sent for the police and when they arrived they were both questioned, about what had happened, and statements were taken.
Bulldog told the police they were both going fishing, when he was shot, and produced his fishing rods, which John had managed to carry, as evidence!
The police told them that they would send someone down to the Mill, to look for evidence.
Finally, after Bulldog's wounds were treated and he was given a painkilling injection, they had to wait a

further hour and a half, f before they were allowed to go home.
John rang for a taxi, and when it arrived, he arranged to drop Bulldog off at the place, where he told John he was living at present, before continuing to his own parent's house!
John's parents wanted to know what had happened, and what he was doing down by Blake's Mill, so the fishing story, was used again as an excuse.
They were obviously concerned by Bulldog being shot, and worried that it could have happened to either of them and maybe killed!
His father was impressed by John's reaction, for getting Bulldog to hospital, and asked if he had any idea who fired the shots!
John replied that he had no idea!

Sitting down later, John felt dismayed by the day's events!

Was the bullet meant for him rather than Bulldog he wondered?

If so why was someone trying to kill him?

Was it the same person who was holding Marion?

CHAPTER 6 - Unexpected Visitor

Having had a restless evening after the events of the day before it was quite late before he went to bed.

So the following morning, John was still in bed when he heard the front doorbell ring.

His father had already left for work so John decided to get up and get dressed, in case there was any more news about Marion.

His mother opened the front door and he heard her talking to the visitor, whoever they were.

He soon lost interest until his mother called him.

"John! Are you up?" She shouted. "There's someone here to see you!"

"I'll be right down Mother!" He replied, hurriedly combing his hair.

He went downstairs and his mother told him his visitor was in the sitting room.

He went in and found there was a man a bit older than his father, dressed in a dark business suit and white collar and tie.

He wore glasses, and his dark hair was receding slightly, at the temples.

"Hello John!" He said carefully extending his hand. "I'm David Ashmore, Marion's father!"

"Pleased to meet you!" Replied John, shaking his hand. "What can I do for you?"

"I wanted to talk to you about my daughters disappearance, John!" He began. "I gather you met Marion again, after the unfortunate incident, of your first encounter. I know Marion, was really upset about your Court appearance, and your subsequent sentencing. She did try, to set things right, and I know you got to meet her in better circumstances, later. She told me about it and believed you got on rather well together! So I also know that she was unhappy, about not being able to see you, during your period of Community Service, of course, but she always hoped, that she might be able to see you, once it was completed. Now she has disappeared, so clutching at straws, I decided to see if there was anything that you might remember, that might explain her absence!"

"I'm so pleased you came!" Said John quickly. "Firstly, I would like to say that, although you might not believe me, I am also devastated about Marion's disappearance, but I must tell you that I certainly had nothing whatsoever to do with it! I knew, and started to believe that we were, slowly becoming more than just good friends."

"I'm pleased to hear that, John!" Said Mr Ashmore quickly. "Marion spoke many times to me, about you, and I believe she began to really care about you. So I think it's unlikely that she would have run away, because of the outcome of your first unfortunate meeting, John! And, of course, I know she didn't, because she's now, been kidnapped!"

"There is one other thing that I still feel bad about!" Said John slowly. "I have never told anyone this, but I saw Marion, on the evening that she disappeared! I guess, apart from the person that took her away, I was the last person to see her. I really feel terrible! You see I should have told the police, but I feel uncomfortable about doing that, after my last appearance!

"Thank you for telling me that, John!" Said Mr Ashmore, gently. "And of course, I can understand your reluctance to tell anyone else that."

"Yes, but I feel such a coward for not revealing it to the police!" Said John. "I lie awake at night wondering if there might have been something that I may have noticed, or forgotten, that may have helped, the police to find her!"

"Strangely enough John, for a different reason, I do the same!" Said Mr Ashmore.

"There is another thing that I haven't revealed though!" Said John carefully. "I also had a phone call, from the man holding Marion, that I didn't tell anyone about! Once again, I feel I should have done so!"

He quickly related the message, that he received, from the mystery caller, plus the result of his subsequent visit to Blake's Mill in Jarvis Avenue.

Mr Ashmore was horrified, when he heard about the shooting, but praised John for the way he dealt with the injury to Bulldog!

"So you believe the person holding Marion was trying to kill you, John!" He said slowly. "This gets worse and worse. The police have to catch him, before he does something even nastier, next time. I think he must be mental!"

"Have you any idea, who he might be, Mr Ashmore?" Asked John quietly. "Did Marion have any old boyfriends, that might be obsessed with her, in some way? What about work colleagues, or old school friends? Or even relatives, or neighbours, etc."

"Once again John, I have been thinking along the same lines!" Said Mr Ashmore. "And please call me David!"

"Thank you David!" Said John, carefully. "It's just that I do tend to think of myself as a total coward, for not revealing my actions and the phone call to the police! That was why I decided to see if I could go and meet the person holding Marion! Stupid, of course, considering I didn't think he would want to kill me! So I apologize, if I've made things worse, by interfereing! I should have kept my nose out of things that don't concern me!"

"Don't blame yourself, John!" Said David quickly. At least you tried to help, and if you hadn't been there your friend Bulldog, could have died!"

"I suppose your right!" Murmured John. "But I still feel wretched! So I'm still hoping, the kidnapper, whoever he or she is, will ring me again!" Added John. "I will do anything he tells me to do, if it will lead to Marion being released!"

"You would do that even if he tried to kill you?" Said David quietly.

"Yes! Of course!" Said John. "I don't think I would want to live without knowing Marion was safe! I suppose that sounds a bit strange, particularly, since we hardly know each other! No David! I'm not getting all misty eyed over your daughter, but now that I've begun to get to know her, I am starting to find that even In such a short time that we spent together, somehow she's become so special to me!"

"Well she's rather special to me too, John!" Said David seriously.

"I agree!" Said John. "But let's look at the little we know about the kidnapper now! First It appears he can ride a motorbike, if he was the one that I saw! It does not mean he owns one though! He also uses a rifle! But may not own one! He is quite small from my recollection of the rider on the motorbike! Could be male or female for the same reason! He sounded male on the phone. But his or her voice could have been disguised. That's all my input!"

"The ransom note was on plain white paper - no watermark!" Said David. "It was written in capitals - no odd letter types! The amount required, 100000 was written once carefully in letters not numbers - therefore no odd numbers or strange pound signs! Paper had a slight perfume odour - could have been sprayed on but perfume was not identified. That's all I have!"

"Okay!" Said John. "Do we have any suspects?"

"Well I don't think it sounds like any of her work colleagues!" Said David. "I have spoken to them all and none of them seem likely - I also understand the Police think they all seem to have alibis. Most of my neighbours are too old or have alibis. Relatives are I hope also unlikely because most of ours do not live locally. Who else do we need to consider?"

"I have been thinking about that!" Said John. "In my case there are a few likely candidates. There are people that I met during my Community Service! People I was at Uni with! Work colleagues! And of course police officers!"

"Yes I didn't consider police officers!" Said David. "Can you pick out any in particular?"

"Well the only ones I remember by name!" Said John. "Were Frank and Jan who arrested me. Unlikely because they were called at random and just happened to be on duty. The only other one of course, was the detective constable who came to my house after Marion's disappearance!"

"The last one is interesting!" Said David. "What was he like?"

"I didn't take too much notice I'm afraid!" Said John. "I suppose he was about 30 to 35, dark hair, about 5 foot 9 or 10, average build! You know, like a normal plain clothes copper!"

"That's interesting!" Said David. "The ones that came to my house were a balding man in his 50's and a young woman! Did you see the man that you saw's warrant card by any chance?"

"Now I think of it! No I didn't! I never thought to ask him!" Said John.

"Well we will have to check up on him!" Said David. "I'll see what I can find out!"

"Well let's see what happens now!" Said John. "Let's hope something turns up! I do hope I get a phone call! If I do, I'll call you and let you know. I'm also going to record it if I can - but I doubt it will be possible to trace it!"

"I'll let you know by phone!" Said David. "If I get any information or hear from the kidnapper! Or receive another Ransom note!"

With that David departed leaving John to try to decide if there was anything else he could do. Since it was now Friday he was not looking forward to spending another weekend without Marion.

An hour later the phone rang.

He rushed to get to it before his mother.

He needn't have worried, because it was Josh.

"Hi John!" Said Josh. "Is it still OK for Monday?"

"Yes! No worries Josh!" Said John. "Everything Okay with you?"

"Of course!" Replied Josh. "By the way! I have been speaking to Bulldog! He is pretty grateful for what you did for him! He would like to help you in your search for the 'low life' that grabbed your girlfriend! The same goes for me as well! Bulldog tells me you went to the old Mill 'cause you got a bell from the scum to go there! He reckons the shooter was aiming for you and got him instead! If he, I mean the scumbag, phones again let me or Bulldog know and we will, this time, be waiting for you to turn up if you are told to go anywhere! Bye!"

Josh rang off and his offer got John thinking.

He spent the rest of the day rigging up an old cassette recorder to the telephone to record any message the kidnapper might give him if he or she rang.

There was no call or other activity on Saturday but on Sunday John rang Josh and asked him if he could find out if any of his or Bulldog's mates could find out anything about the person on the motorbike, that he described.

On Monday morning David Ashmore rang to say that they had received another ransom letter with further demands for money.

At 11 o'clock Josh arrived for his reading lesson.

When John opened the door Josh had a bunch of letters in his hand.

"Your Postie's late round here!" He said. "He gave me these when he saw me coming up your path!"

He handed over the mail which John glanced through.

Most of the letters were for one or other of his parents, but the last one was addressed to him.

He opened it carefully and found a single page sheet of A4 paper with a lock of hair attached to it!

The writing on the sheet said:-

This is a piece of your friend Marion. If you want the rest of her, you must do as you're told. Why did you turn up with that idiot that I shot. Oh don't worry, no one recognised Sir Arthur Westerfields son Gareth, who you know as Bulldog. The temptation to put a bullet through his puny brain was almost too much for me. So I messed up my real purpose which was to end your miserable existence John. Now you are going to provide me with another chance if you wish to exchange your life for that of your lady friend Marion. To do so you must come alone to the top of Devil Rock at 3 o'clock on Monday. I will be waiting for you there and only one of us will come down! If it's me Marion will not die so for her sake it had better not be you!

John folded the paper and replaced it in the envelope.

"Where is Devil Rock Josh?" Asked John.

"It's over by the side of the hill where they do Para-gliding at weekends!" Said Josh. "Devil's Rock is the name of the cliff where the base jumpers leap off. It's pretty high! You don't intend to go there on Monday do you John? You'll be killed for sure if you are pushed off there. And we won't be able to wait for you and him up there. There's no cover!"

"It certainly looks difficult!" Said John. "But I will have to go and meet whoever it is that's holding Marion. I have no choice!"

"So me and my mates have seven days to locate this scumbag or find anywhere your friend Marion is being kept." Said Josh. "I had better go and see what they have found. So I guess I will have to wait a bit longer for you to teach me to read John! The bit about Bulldog was interesting - if it's true! I'll have to ask him! Do you think he might know who the person who recognised him is?"

"I don't know what to think Josh!" Said John. "Except I must do something to rescue Marion! She must be terrified by now!"

"We will go and try to sort something out for you John!" Said Josh. "See you!"

After Josh left John began analysing his present situation.

He began to review the facts as they now appeared.

The interesting info regarding Bulldog was a bit of a surprise.

Was it true?

If so why did the letter include it?

Did it matter anyway as far as he was concerned?

Who was the detective that called at his house?

Was he a real one or not?

Was David Ashmore actually the real David Ashmore? His mother must have met him so she obliviously must have known who he was!

Who was the rider on the motorbike?

Was it a woman?

If so which woman?

Could it even be Marion?

Why was he, John, being targeted anyway?

After all he was nobody special?

Was the person on the motorbike the person that shot Bulldog?

Or was there someone else in the Mill?

Why did Bulldog just happen to be there at the same time as he was there?

What is all this about anyway?

Was Marion really a clever actress with no interest in him apart from revenge for their first encounter?

He really hoped that was not the case, but it could not just be dismissed!

He was left with several things that he needed to clarify.

1. Talk to Bulldog.

2. Check David Ashmore. Not likely to be a problem but you never know!

3. Check detective.

4. Find background of Marion
5. Investigate Blake's Mill.
6. Look at Devil's Rock.
7. Find out why someone wants him dead.

Of course the main thing he needed to do is work out why he had been set up in the first place and by who.

One thing was certain he was not going anywhere near Devil's Rock!!

CHAPTER 7 - Bulldog and Blake's Mill

He decided at first to go and see Bulldog or whoever he really is!

He had to wait for a couple of days to allow Bulldog to recover from his injury.

There was still no news about Marion and the Ashmores had not heard anything more from the kidnapper!

Eventually, early on Wednesday morning, he called a taxi and went to the address where before, he had dropped Bulldog off after they left the hospital.

When he arrived he found himself outside a block of flats with a problem, since he did not know which one Bulldog might live in!

Also since he only knew him as Bulldog, rather than whatever his real name might be who should he ask for?

However he now saw there was a young boy kicking a football about in front of the flats.

John decided to take a risk and ask him anyway, so he called to him.

"Is there anyone living here that calls himself Bulldog?" He asked.

The boy thought for a moment before replying.

"Yes mister!" He said. "You must be thinking about Old Miss George's lodger! Up on the second floor!"

John thanked the boy and headed for the main door.

On the wall inside there were a number of small mail lockers, each with names on them.

He looked through them and found one marked Mrs George and a flat number on the second floor as the boy had said.

He made his way to an area with a couple of lifts!

They both had labels stuck on them saying 'Out of Order', so he took the stairs to the second floor instead.

Once there he walked along a corridor until he arrived at Mrs Georges door and rang the bell.

After a short delay the door was partly opened on a chain, revealing an elderly woman with curlers in her hair.

"What do you want?" She asked suspiciously.

"I was looking for a friend of mine called Bulldog!" John replied politely.

"Oh!" She said. "Who wants him?"

"I'm John!" Replied John.

"Hold on! I'll see if he's in!" She said and shut the door.

Five minutes later the door was opened fully, without the chain, and Bulldog stood there.

"Hi John!" Said Bulldog warmly. "Good to see you! Come in!"

He led John to a room in the flat that was obviously his.

"Sit down John!" Said Bulldog.

"How's the shoulder now! I see you have lost the sling!" Said John

"Yes! It was a bloody nuisance! The shoulder still feels a bit sore but at least I can move my arm OK now!" Said Bulldog.

"That's good!" Said John. "It was lucky for me you were there, but not for you of course! Sorry Bulldog! I didn't put that very well! But you know what I meant!"

"Yes I guess your right John!" Said Bulldog with a grin. "I hadn't been down there for quite a while, being otherwise engaged as you know, but I wish I had chosen a different day for fishing!"

"I know it's none of my business!" Asked John. "But where did you get the name Bulldog!"

"It's no secret John!" Bulldog laughed. "As Josh told you, It's not a good idea to use your real name when you are doing Community Service! My real name is Walter Handley, and I come from Nottingham! I was down here doing a Job - no not that kind, a proper job as a Shipping Clerk! Of course I lost that when I had a bit of trouble with some 'friends' of mine and got arrested! You know the rest! My family have rather disowned me for giving them a bad name! Now having a Criminal Record has ruined my chances of getting a decent job again!"

"I'm in the same situation Bulldog, or should I call you Walter!" Said John.

"Round here I prefer Bulldog!" Said Bulldog. "You see Its a bit of a rough neighbourhood and the name gives me a bit of what Josh calls street cred!"

"I'm in a bit of bother as well!" Said John. "It seems I must have upset someone, which is why they want to kill me!"

"Can I help in any way?" Asked Bulldog. "Not to kill you, of course! I owe you one after what you did for me! No I mean to help you find the scumbag whose trying to knock you off!"

"I can think of one small thing!" Said John. "How did you get to the bottom of Jarvis Avenue without walking all the way down it. I would like to have a look round the old Mill without drawing too much attention to it."

"That's no problem!" He said quickly. "I'll take you there now if you like, using my short cut. Let me get a torch and my coat and we'll go right now!"

"What about your shoulder?" Said John.

"It doesn't stop me walking John!" Said Bulldog with a grin. "But don't ask me to do too much weight lifting! Let's go!"

Bulldog told Mrs George he was going out and grabbed his key and a torch and led John out of the flats!

Bulldog led John, along a number of roads and eventually across a couple of fields, until they finally emerged from the wood opposite the Mill.

There was no signs of anyone around, so they looked both ways to make sure before crossing the deserted road, and making their way round the side of the old mill building.

The door at the side was locked and bolted but Bulldog soon found a window at the back that was broken.

They carefully removed some of the glass to avoid cutting themselves, before opening it fully!

They climbed carefully inside and looked around, finding themselves in a small room overlooking the river.

Outside the window they could see where the water wheel would once have been turned by a now disused mill race.

Using Bulldogs torch, they saw that the room they were in, was empty, so they crossed it to a door which led to other rooms and also a staircase!

John led the way, as they went carefully up the stairs, which were in a poor state of repair.

The rooms upstairs were all empty, but they could see that the one at the front of the building had no window, but had been used recently, because the floor was swept clean.

They returned downstairs and began to search the rooms there.

They eventually found one at the front, which was not only swept clean but also had a window facing the wood.

Bulldog thought this was probably the one, from where the shots had been fired.

There was nothing in the room and, as Bulldog said, the Police must have searched it anyway!

They tried the other rooms on this floor, most of which were also empty!

However moving to the one on the left of the staircase, John stepped on an old worn carpet and felt the floor move.

He quickly pulled back the carpet, to reveal, set in the floor, a heavy trapdoor, the hinges of which appeared to be newly oiled.

Between them John and the injured Bulldog, just managed with difficulty, to lift it up, revealing a set of stone steps leading downwards into the darkness.

Once again, Bulldog took out the small torch that he had thoughtfully brought with him, and led the way carefully as they descended the steps slowly!

At the bottom they found a short tunnel, a few yards long, at the end of which there was a stout door with heavy bolts at the top and bottom.

They saw that the bolts were also newly greased, so they drew each of them, back gently and John slowly opened the door.

They were greeted by the sight of Marion, lying fully clothed, but uncovered, on a small camp bed, unconscious.

Her wrists had been handcuffed and the cuffs were, in turn, chained to a metal plate attached to the wall!

The blankets, that should have covered her and kept her warm, were lying in a heap on the floor, beside the camp bed.

John noticed that the blankets had obviously overturned a small table, which clearly must have held some food and water, the remains of which was scattered on the floor!

John went over to Marion, and hurriedly felt her neck for her pulse.

"She's cold, but still breathing, at least!" Announced John, reaching down for one of the blankets to cover her up.

"It seems to me, that she is more than just asleep, Bulldog!" Stated John. "She may have been drugged! So I think we need something, to lever the panel attach!ed to the chains, off the wall! The handcuffs are locked on her wrists so I can't get them off."

"You stay with her,? John, while i go and try to find something we can use." Said Bulldog.

He returned quickly with a rusty iron bar, which they managed between them, to use to lever the metal plate, to which the chains were attached, off the wall!

John, then managed to lift the sleeping Marion, with the chains and metal plate, still handcuffed to her wrists, off the camp bed!

With a little help from the injured Bulldog, they managed to carry her plus the plate and chains, with some difficulty, back up the stone steps.

Bulldog went down to retrieve one of the blankets, to cover Marion and try to keep her warm!

Once there, they shut the trapdoor and replaced the carpet, before managing to manoeuvre Marion and chains, carefully and gently out of the room and over to the broken window!

There was a difficult few minutes as they manoeuvred Marion with the plate and chains, through the window!

Once outside, .John carried her gently down to a place by the river, covered her with the blanket, and splashed some water gently on her face.

She slowly opened her eyes slightly, and groaned.

When John looked at her in the daylight, he could see where her hair had been cut to provide the sample that had been sent to him.

She was still affected by whatever she had been drugged with, so she did not manage to keep her eyes open or wake up.

"We have to get her away from here, as soon as possible!" John remarked. "In case, whoever left her in there, comes back! If you can lead the way, I'll have to carry her."

They crossed the road and John struggled, to carry the unconscious Marion, still with the chains attached to her wrists, into the wood.

He had to put her down for a moment, before carrying her to the other side of the trees!

Luckily, on the other side of the wood, there was a meadow with short grass.

Thankfully, It was dry, so John laid her down gently, covered her up again and massaged her wrists and arms, which were still marked by the chains handcuffed to her wrists.

She opened her eyes again briefly, but quickly closed them again, in the sunlight.

"Her eyes aren't used to the light, after all that time in the darkness!" Said Bulldog quietly, taking off his jacket and covering her up.

"Thank you so much Bulldog, for helping me today!" Said John. "Especially with your injured shoulder! This has been the best day I have had for a long time! All I need to do now is get her safely home and remove the chains!"

"If she has a hairpin in her hair, or a safety pin, John! I believe I may be able to undo the handcuffs!" Said Bulldog quietly.

John felt gently through her hair but found nothing, and found that there were no safety pins in her clothes either.

Bulldog was not going to be beaten however, and he found an old piece of chicken wire, in one of the hedges!

After a lot of bending, he managed to extract a small piece, which he used to finally unlock and remove, first one and then the other of her handcuffs!

John therefore, having got rid of the chains, picked Marion up in his arms and bit by bit carried her across the fields and over a couple of fences, onto a road!

Halfway along the road, a white van driver, seeing them struggling with Marion, stopped and asked if they needed any help.

John told him, Marion had fainted, and was not feeling very well.

He asked the driver if he knew where Marion's road was.

He did!

So John and Bulldog lifted her into the van which was luckily, unloaded and with Bulldog in the front, and John in the back, cradling Marion in his arms, the van driver, drove them all back to her road.

Helped by Bulldog and the van driver, John lifted Marion out of the van, and carried her to what he hoped, was her house.

It wasn't!

It was the one next door, but the woman in it, went next door and Marion's mother, came and assisted John, to carry her daughter back into her own house.

John laid her gently on a settee in the Sitting room, and stroked her hair and face, while Bulldog sat down, feeling tired, on one of the armchairs.

Marion's mother was naturally, in tears, at seeing her daughter again, but immediately rang for the doctor and also her husband, who she said, was still as work.

Before the doctor arrived, Marion opened her eyes, and looked uncertainly round her sitting room.

"How did I get here?" She said sleepily.

Her eyes settled on John, who was sitting beside her, and she began to cry!

"I've missed you so much!" She sobbed holding one of his hands tightly. "Please don't leave me again!"

John kissed her gently on the forehead, and quietly told her to rest.

Marion's father, David was first to arrive!

John was pleased to see that he was the same David that he had seen before and not an imposter!

David rang the police, to inform them that Marion had been found, and rescued!

He was followed shortly afterwards by the doctor who immediately began to examine Marion!

John left them alone, while he thanked Bulldog for his help, and walked with him to the van, where the driver was waiting patiently having agreed to take him home.

"Please come and see me tomorrow Bulldog if you can." Said John. "We still have some work to do but thanks a million for your help today!"

Having thanked the driver who set off, John returned to Marion's house.

The doctor said he could not tell what substances she might have been given, but he had taken some blood samples for analysis.

He said Marion had told him she had been given food and drink during her captivity, so physically she didn't appear to be too badly affected by her ordeal!

He said he would call back in the morning to check on Marion and suggested she would benefit from a good night's sleep after her experience.

He left a prescription for some cream to treat the marks on her wrists and arms and quickly left.

Marion's parents were naturally overjoyed to have their daughter back safely.

Both of them hugged and thanked John, who phoned his mother to let her know what had happened.

He said he ought to leave them now to allow them to look after Marion.

Marion however had other ideas.

"Please don't leave me yet John!" She said quietly, with a smile. "I can't bear losing you even for a moment now we are together again"

Her mother said John could stay and have some tea and sandwiches if he wished.

She added that she had rung Johns parents and invited them to join them here.

John's mother came to join them and said his father was on his way home from work, having heard the news!

Marion refused to let go of Johns hand as they all finally had a quiet meal together.

A little later Marion's mother got up and escorted her daughter up to bed.

John and his parents said their goodbyes and prepared to leave.

Marion's mother came down and said Marion begged her to ask if John could go upstairs to say goodnight.

He asked her mother's permission before he went up, and found her nestled down in her bed with her favourite childhood Teddy Bear nestled in her arms!

He leaned over and kissed her gently.

"Goodnight sweetheart!" He said gently and prepared to leave. "Go to sleep now and I'll see you tomorrow!"

"Don't go yet John!" She whispered quietly. "Promise you will come back!"

"Of course I will come back!" Said John with a smile. "I have to! Tomorrow I would like to ask your father if I can marry his daughter!"

"Do you really mean that John!" She said gently, with a wicked frown. "Don't you think you ought to ask his daughter first!"

"I was going to!" He laughed. "But I was afraid she might run a mile at the thought!"

"Well ask me now and find out!" She said looking serious.

"Okay!" Said John holding her hand and kneeling down. "Marion! Will you do me the honour of becoming my wife!"

"I'll have to think about it!" She teased, before saying. "The answers a gorgeous Yes! Yes! Yes!"

She leaned over and kissed him.

"Thank you for that!" He said. "Now I must go or your dad will throw me out!"

"Just one more minute John!" She said calling out. "Mum can you come here for a moment?"

Her mother who was waiting outside, came in.

"John's asked me to be his wife mum!" Marion said happily. "And I have said Yes!"

"I'm really happy for you both dear!" Said her mother with a smile. "But now you must get some sleep dear."

"And I must go too!" Said John gently. "If it's OK with everyone I will see you in the morning. Sleep well! Goodnight!"

John left and went home to tell his parents that they were going to have a new Daughter in Law!

John finally tumbled into bed and slept happily for the first time in several days.

CHAPTER 8 - Unfinished Business

In the morning John got up early and went round to Marion's house as soon as it was reasonable to do so.

He found Marion up and dressed.

She had washed her hair and she told him she had had a shower as well!

She was now wearin seeg a red sweater over a navy blue pleated skirt.

Even without a trace of makeup she looked stunning as she sat on the settee.

John went over and kissed her.

"You seemed to have scrubbed up pretty well." He teased. "How are you this morning dear?"

"Rather better than I was yesterday morning!" She replied with a smile. "Thanks to my future husband and his friend!"

"Has your doctor been back to see you?" Asked John.

"Yes! And he has said I am OK now!" Said Marion brightly. "Apparently the only thing that I had been given was some kind of sleeping tablet, so I have not become a drug addict anyway! He said I could go out today if I feel up to it!"

"That sounds better Marion!" Said John. "But from now on I never intend to let you out of my sight, even for a moment!"

"I must go out today though John!" Marion said gently.

"Where do you want to go!" Said a puzzled looking John.

"Into town of course!" She teased. "I want to go somewhere for you to choose me an engagement ring straight away - in case you change your mind!"

"Why would I do that after you have made me the happiest man in the world!" He said with a smile. "I wish I had one now for you! Before I do anything else now I have to go and have a word with your father!"

John went into the next room to find her father, who was sitting reading the daily paper.

"May I have a word with you David, I mean Mr Ashmore!" John said seriously.

"Of course John!" Said David putting down his paper and getting up.

"May I have your permission to marry your daughter!" He said.

"I suppose I should now ask about your prospects etc." Smiled David. "But I already know how you feel about her! So I am overjoyed that you are going to be my future Son-in-Law John! Of course you have my permission."

He reached out and shook John's hand vigorously.

"Thank you Mr Ashmore!" Said John.

Marion, who had been listening outside the door, ran in and flung her arms around her father and kissed him.

"Thank you Daddy." She said happily. "I do love you!"

"Shouldn't you be saying that to your Fiancée rather than me!" Her father said.

"Oh! I do like the sound of that Daddy." She said throwing her arms round John and kissing him.

Marion's mother, who had also been listening came in and hugged John and her daughter.

"Now I can tell everyone, can't I David?" She said excitedly. "And we can plan your wedding Marion and John!"

"I have to find a special ring for my Fiancée first of all!" Said John quietly, holding Marion's hand. "I'll go home and get my coat and perhaps we can go into town."

John went back to his house and put on his coat.

CHAPTER 9 - Surprise for John

Before he could leave the phone rang.

John picked up the receiver humming to himself quietly.

"Hello!" He said.

"Hello John." Said a voice that John recognised. "Sorry to spoil your excitement, but you forget that we have an appointment on Monday at 3 o'clock. Yes I know you have unfortunately got your lady friend back! In fact I am looking at her right now."

John went to the window and looked out

"It's no use trying to see me John, I am too far away!" Said the voice. "But I can see you - these Telescopic Sights are marvellous!"

"So why don't you shoot me now and get it over with." Said John.

"Oh no John!" Said the voice. "That's no fun! You must keep your appointment with me up on Devil Rock."

"What if I refuse?" Said John.

"I'm looking at your lady now!" He said. "So listen!"

He heard the sound of a gun going off in the phones earpiece then a click as the phone went dead.

He rushed back to Marion's house.

When he got there he could see the lounge window was smashed.

He ran up the path and looked through the broken window.

Marion was in an armchair holding her face.

He banged on the door till her mother opened it, then ran past her into the lounge!

Marion was still sitting in the chair and beside her on the table there was the shattered remains of a glass vase.

He ran to her and saw her cheek was bleeding.

He swept her up in his arms and carried her out of the room into the kitchen which was at the back of the house.

Her mother had followed John into the kitchen and was soon dabbing at Marion's cheek with a tissue.

"Are you alright darling?" Said John,

"Yes! I think so!" Said Marion shivering. "Something hit my face when the vase exploded! I don't know what happened! I think someone threw something through our front window because it was broken too!"

"I'm afraid it was a bullet that did that!" Said John.

He explained about the telephone call.

"It looks like the person that kidnapped you is still around and dangerous." He said. "He still expects me to meet him on Devil's Rock on Monday! So now I have no choice! I will have to go and get it over with dear! I cannot have him hurting you!"

"But that's in four days time!" Said Marion tearfully.

"Yes I know darling!" Said John gently. "So we still have 3 days together at least. If I don't come back on Monday you will know I always loved you! But I am hoping I can do something to change the mad man's mind about killing me. Either way I have to know you won't be harmed!"

"But without you I would not want to go on John." Said Marion, with tears in her eyes. "You are the most important thing in my life now and you always will be."

She put her arms around Johns neck and wept on his shoulder.

CHAPTER 10 - Bulldog's Visit!

They both jumped as the doorbell rang.

David went and answered it.

"Someone to see you John!" He called.

John went to the front door and found Bulldog standing there.

He had forgotten that he had asked Bulldog to come and see him today.

"Hi Bulldog !" He said cheerfully. "Thanks again for yesterday!"

"I noticed the window is smashed as I came up the path!" Said Bulldog. "What happened to it?"

"Oh just a little present from our former kidnap nutter!" Said John. "I guess he was a bit upset when he discovered Marion had gone!"

"That's not all though!" Said Marion, who had come to see who had called. "He still wants John to meet him on Devil's Rock! John will be killed if he falls or gets pushed off there!"

"You didn't tell me that he was still intent on bumping you off John!" Said Bulldog in horror. "You can't be thinking of going up to Devil's Rock are you? It would be suicide! The man's clearly off his head!"

"I know!" Said John with a sigh. "But someone has to stop him before he does something worse and someone does gets killed. He took a shot as Marion just now, that's why the windows broken!"

"Well you are not going up to Devil's Rock John!" Said Bulldog strongly. "If anyone goes it will be me! I owe him one for shooting me already! I would love the chance to wring his rotten neck!"

"It's not your problem Bulldog!" Said John gently. "It's mine!"

"Well there may be a way out yet!" Said Bulldog. "Josh and I are on the case now! We will think of something John! I'm not letting you go up to Devil's Rock alone! I'm off now to see Josh and his brother and a few more people! See you both in a couple of days! Promise you won't do anything silly till then John!"

He turned on his heel and departed!

John went back indoors with a sad looking Marion!

"Don't worry dear!" He said seriously. "I'm not dead yet and I don't intend to be!"

On Friday John had made up his mind to escort Marion into town to buy her an engagement ring as he had promised her!

At first she was too worried about John going up to Devil's Rock on Monday, but she cheered up slightly when they got to the first of several jewellers in the town centre!

John insisted they should not choose the first ring that they saw, but should look at all the ones in all the jewellers before deciding which one for her to choose!

They finally after a long morning, decided on the ring that Marion wanted and John purchased it for her!

She could not have it straight away, because it needed to be altered to her size, so John took her to the café that they first went to (and the one he went to the morning after Marion was kidnapped) for a quick bite to eat!

In the afternoon they went back to the jewellers that were altering her ring and collected it!

John put it on her third finger and gave her the ring box before taking her home to show her parents!

They had already decided to spend the weekend together quietly at Marion's house!

Marion's parents, David and Sue, had also invited John's parents for Sunday lunch, so that they could all celebrate John and Marion's engagement!

John and Marion spent a quiet and restful Saturday in each other's company, before on Sunday, as arranged, they enjoyed a pleasant Sunday Lunch with both of their parents!

After lunch, David opened a bottle of Champagne and everyone toasted the happy pair!

CHAPTER 11 - Josh & Bulldog's Plans

At 4 o'clock on Sunday afternoon there was a knock on the door and Bulldog arrived again!

Marion's father opened the door and took Bulldog into the sitting room to meet John!

"Hi Bulldog!" Said John. "How's the shoulder now?"

"Oh its miles better now thanks!" Replied Bulldog seriously. "I hope you have changed your mind about going up to Devil's Rock on Monday John!"

"No Bulldog!" Said John gently. "I have to see this thing through! I can't risk anything happening to Marion!"

"I still think you ought to let me go instead of you John!" Said Bulldog!

"As I have said it's not your problem!" Replied John. "It's become mine!"

"Well in that case I have a few things that might help!" Said Bulldog! "What I haven't told you is that yesterday I went back to the old Mill with Josh, to see if there was anything that we might have missed when we rescued Marion. As you know, the police had been there so we didn't expect to find anything in the Mill! We looked round anyway and nothing had changed there, but down by the river, we found a small shed that must once have been something to do with the Mill. It had no windows and Its door was padlocked by a new lock! However once again we found that the hinges on the door had been oiled or greased! Josh picked the lock (one of his party tricks from when he was a burglar)! Inside we were surprised to find a Para-Glider - you know one of the things with an oblong parachute instead of a wing, and an engine and propeller. We thought It could mean the nutter is intending to use it to go up to Devil's Rock and then presumably to escape after his encounter with you!"

"That's interesting!" Said John. "But how am I going to combat that! I guess he could turn up on that, shoot me, then fly off and escape."

"Well Josh and I, had worked that one out as well!" Said Bulldog. "So we decided to try to find a way to upset his plans! Of course we could have just destroyed the Para-Glider, so he wouldn't be able to use it! But we realised that would mean he could just get another one, change the time and still turn up or find another way to target you! So we sat down and worked out a way of sabotaging the machine, so that it would get him up to Devil's Rock but not down again. We decided finally to work on the parachute. There were two thick cords on each end, attached to a seat which had a harness attached to it to be worn by the pilot. We partially cut through one of the cords on one end of the parachute and ensured it would not be noticed when it was used! It should take some time to pull apart but when it does the parachute will come loose so it will not fly. We could not find a way of sabotaging the engine though or the propeller! I guess It's not much of a plan but we thought it might help!"

"Yes it might give me some hope I guess!" Said John. "But It would be nice to have a weapon of some kind! Not that anything is going to be any use against a rifle is it?"

"Josh and I thought about that too John!" Said Bulldog. "But as you just said, there's not much you could use against a rifle. So we looked at the possibility of a shield rather than a weapon. We didn't think a metal shield of any kind would be any use against a rifle either, because a bullet would go straight through it. However, later, when we were talking to Josh's big brother Nat, he came up with a possible solution! It turned out he's an Arsenal football supporter - no neither am I John! But he told Josh and me that once at an away game in Turkey, that he went to last year, the game was nearly abandoned because some of the Turkish supporters, let off smoke bombs! The smoke blew across the pitch so no one could see the ball, forcing the Ref to take the teams off until the smoke cleared."

"I see what you mean!" Said John. "But I can't take a smoke bomb up there with me, and even if I could It would not cause much of a fog up there and it would soon disperse in the wind anyway!"

"Yes that's right!" Said Bulldog. "If you only had one! But Josh's brother has obtained about a dozen (don't ask me where from) and they are the type that the Army use on manoeuvres. They have detonators that can be fired remotely when triggered from something like a Smart Phone! At this moment Josh and his Brother's gang are burying them around the top of the hill by Devil's Rock. His Brother is a bit of an electronics whiz kid, so he's working on rigging the bombs remote timing devices so they will go off in sequence when they get a signal from this phone!"

Bulldog took a phone out of his packet and gave it to John.

"Josh's brother has said he will set the phone up for you before you go up there and explain how to use it!" Said Bulldog. "He told us it uses a similar programme that terrorists use to set off car bombs (again don't ask me where he got that info from)! But if it all works, it should then make the hill almost impossible for the smart-arse kidnapper to see you, and I suppose you to see him. What you do then I don't know I'm afraid, but it's the best we could come up with! And of course the smoke bomb setup hasn't been tested, for obvious reasons! And once again I still wish you would let me go up there in your place."

"Thanks for all that!" Said John giving Bulldog a hug! "And make sure you thank Josh and his brother Nat!"

Bulldog said he was not going anywhere so he would return and wait with John tomorrow, to show him where Devil's Rock was, and try and persuade him to change his mind!

John really thought this was all madness and unlikely to work, but he didn't wish to say so to Bulldog! But he was grateful for the efforts of his friends for at least trying to help him.

Although he thought that he had little or no chance against the maniac with the gun, he still believed he had no option other than meeting his opponent up on the hill!

He thought his only faint hope was, that in some way, he could persuade his opponent to think again, rather than trying to kill him!

It still seemed unlikely to succeed, since Marion had already been targeted the other morning, but it was all he could think of!

CHAPTER 12 - Devil's Rock

Marion, her mother and David, for their part, all wanted to get the police involved, but John said it would only scare off the maniac for a while.

It would still leave them all at the killers mercy with the chance to target any of them at any time with his long range rifle.

No! He had to be stopped somehow now, and he believed he was the only person able to do it!

Also he thought it would be difficult for the police to take any action now, because there was no clue to the madman's identity.

Finally at 2 o'clock John kissed Marion and set off for his meeting with his opponent up on Devil's Rock.

Of course he had never been there so he needed Bulldog to show him the way.

They both arrived at 2 thirty at the bottom of the steep path up to the hill top and

Josh and his brother were there to meet them!

Josh's brother took John's phone, made some adjustments and checked a few things before returning it!

He explained which button to press and told John to wait as long as possible before triggering the smoke bombs!

Josh gave John a baseball bat and a knife to use if he managed to get near enough to his opponent to use them!

Bulldog tried for a final time, without success, to get John to let him take his place and lastly, they all wished John good luck as he set off to climb the path up to Devil's Rock!

When he got there he looked around to get his bearings!

He could not see where the smoke bombs were concealed and he did not want to get too near to the edge of the drop to the valley below!

He looked at his watch!

It said 2 fifty six!

He looked around for signs of the Para-Glider that he had been told to expect!

He couldn't see anything at first, but then he heard the sound of an engine below the far side of the hill!

As the sound of the engine drew louder, the oblong parachute appeared first about 150 yards away, rising upwards until he could see the passenger suspended below it!

He was strapped to a seat on the fuselage that supported the engine and the propeller which were mounted behind his seat!

The man was dressed all in black and was wearing a black helmet and dark goggles!

As the craft got nearer, John could see that the pilot was armed with a pistol instead of the rifle that John was expecting, presumably because the rifle would be too difficult to hold, aim and fire while controlling his flying machine!

John realised the pistol would be less accurate than the rifle so he needed to keep moving about to provide a more difficult target!

As the Para-Glider drew nearer the man started firing at him, but no bullets came near him!

The machine was soon just above the hill and started coming quickly nearer!

He saw the man looking downwards to find a suitable landing place!

John took out the phone and pressed the appropriate button as he had been shown!

At first nothing happened, then there was a bang to his right followed by a cloud of black smoke!

He saw the man jump in surprise and his machine wobbled!

There was a second bang on Johns left and more smoke arose!

The man clearly began to realise that it was becoming harder to see the ground!

A third bang from the right released more smoke and John was also finding it more difficult to see!

The man, realising that, because of the smoke, he couldn't land safely, pulled his machine up above the smoke as yet another bang came from the left!

Still climbing he flew 10 feet over Johns head and John threw himself flat as the machine flew out over the edge of Devils Rock!

The Para-Glider was now about 100 feet higher than where John was standing!

John could see the man was trying to turn it round to come back, when John heard a loud snap and saw one end of the oblong parachute fly upwards and deflate!

The man obviously also saw what had happened, and John saw him release his harness and reach for his chest!

John realised he was wearing an emergency parachute and he had pulled the rip cord!

The small drogue chute flew straight back through the metal mesh barrier surrounding the propeller and caught in the blades!

The propeller stopped and the man's emergency parachute emerged from its pack and became tangled in the remains of the oblong parachute that should have provided the lift!

This caused the machine to begin to spin and drop rapidly towards the ground below!

As it fell he heard the screams from the man as he realised he was then doomed!

Finally man and machine hit the ground together and the glider's fuselage disintegrated!

The fuel tank must have been ruptured in the impact, because he could see that fire had broken out in the wreckage!

While John was engrossed in watching the demise of his opponent, he began to be aware of another engine coming from somewhere on his left!

He saw a Microlight aircraft emerge from behind the hill, flying quickly down towards the burning crash!

It was being flown by a figure also wearing black, and it looked as though it was going to try and land by the wreckage!

It looked initially as if it would succeed, but the pilot tried to turn the plane at the last minute and because it was too low, one wingtip hit the ground!

The plane cart wheeled and broke up!

The pilot was thrown clear and John thought at first he was OK, but when he came to rest John could see that there was something red sticking out of the middle of his body!

He had clearly become impaled on a piece of the wrecked plane!

The next thing he saw was Josh and Bulldog and their friends running towards the two wrecks!

So he began to carefully make his way through the smoke which was still being released from the remaining smoke bombs!

He eventually managed to find the path and carefully make his way slowly down from the hill.

When he arrived at the bottom, he found Bulldog had come back to report that there were no survivors from the two machines!

Bulldog also told him that strangely they discovered that the pilot of the Microlight was a woman!

He also said that Josh's brother had rung the police to report the 'accident'!

Bulldog said he told the police on his phone that he thought the two machines collided and came down together!

Josh and his brother and their friends were waiting by the wreckage, for the police to arrive!

Bulldog said he had come back to tell John to go home before the police got there, to avoid any awkward questions about his presence there!

John said he had left the baseball bat and knife that Josh had given him up on the hill!

Bulldog told him not to worry because someone was going up there to remove the remainder of the smoke bombs etc. anyway!

John therefore took Bulldog's advice and left, after asking him to call in at Marion's house later to let him know how they got on with the police etc.!

John hurried back from the hill to one of the nearby roads and from there he arrived, half an hour later at Marion's house.

Before he got to the front door it was opened and Marion ran out and flung herself into John's arms and kissed him.

"I'm so pleased to see you darling!" She said breathlessly. "I have been so worried about you!"

"I'm rather glad to be here as well!" Replied John. "I thought that I was not going to survive when I was waiting up on the hill! It was only my love for you that made me determined to overcome and survive the meeting with the sick maniac up there!"

"Come inside John!" Said Marion quickly, looking around her fearfully.

"Don't worry dear!" Said John, hugging her tightly. "It's all over now! So you and I can relax again!"

"Does that mean you killed him then John?" She said gently.

"No I didn't! But he is certainly dead!" Said John. "Let's go inside and I'll tell you all that happened up there!"

They walked back to the house where John found his and Marion's parents waiting together in the dining room at the back of the house.

Marion and John sat down holding hands while John told them what had occurred up on the hill and finally below it, including the death of the man and woman.

John's father was pleased that John had not actually killed the man in person, even though he realised his death was probably caused by Josh and Bulldog sabotaging the man's parachute!

The death of the woman was her own fault of course, so John did not have a hand in that.

For his part John did not regret the death of the man responsible for the kidnap and shooting of Marion!

If he had not been killed it could have been himself at the bottom of Devil's Rock and Marion would still have been in danger.

He still wanted to know the identity of the dead man and discover what reason the man had for wanting to kill him!

He also needed to know what connection the woman, who also died, had to the man - was she part of the conspiracy waged by the man or just an innocent bystander influenced by the man in some way.

John hoped Bulldog or Josh might have learnt something from the police.

David said he expected the police would let him know that the man suspected of kidnapping Marion was now dead, if he is of course, identified as the one responsible!

If not, he guessed they would either say nothing or tell him that they have no idea who is responsible for Marion's kidnap.

Marion on the other hand was merely hugely relieved that John had survived and come back in one piece.

"I'm sorry someone had to die!" She said, still hugging John. "But I could not have lived without you John! Although we have only known each other for just over 6 months I feel as if we were destined to be together and I could never love anyone else now!"

"I feel the same Marion!" John replied, kissing her. "Now that it's safe to go out we must go into town! Then we must sit down and decide when we are going to get married!"

"If you two lovebirds don't mind!" Said David with a smile. "Can I just say something? Come here Sue!"

Marion's mother walked over to her husband.

"My wife and I have looked forward for 25 years to our daughter getting married!" Continued David. "I hope you aren't thinking of denying us the pleasure of planning the Wedding. Don't worry John! We always said we did not want a big do with hundreds of guests. We wanted, and we still want, you both to decide what you want and who the guests should be. If you want a simple do with just a handful of people there, or a big do it's up to you both to decide"

"Thanks Dad and Mum." Said Marion quickly. "That's good of you both. But at least we managed to get properly engaged first. I thought at one time John might change his mind if I didn't get a ring on my finger! Mighten you have John?"

"There was no chance of that happening, dear!" Said John with a wink. "But you might have got a better offer if I didn't grab you!"

"How could I find anyone better than you?" Said Marion squeezing his hand.

"Ok!" Laughed Sue and David together. "I think we get the message! Now let's all celebrate John's survival on Devil's Rock!"

CHAPTER 13 - Into Town & Bulldog's Report

So the following morning Marion and John caught the bus into town, because Marion wanted to take the opportunity to drop in at the Law firm in the high street where she was employed as a Legal Secretary! She had been on unpaid leave since being kidnapped so she wanted to find out if she still had a job to come back to now that things were hopefully returning to normal!

She was pleased to learn firstly that her job had been kept open for her to return if she felt able after her experience!

Secondly her employer informed her that she had been granted special leave due to unforeseen circumstances, which meant that she would receive all of her usual pay on her next monthly pay day!

Thirdly she was asked if John was with her and if so could he come and see her employer!

She went out and invited John, who was still waiting outside, to come in!

He followed her in and was asked to sit down while one of the firm's Solicitors was sent for!

When he arrived he shook hands with John, before informing him that the case against him had been dismissed and his sentence therefore deemed unlawful!

His criminal record had therefore been removed and his DNA sample had been destroyed!

As a result a claim for compensation had been filed and accepted thus entitling him to the sum of ten thousand pounds!
He was handed a check for this amount and told that the legal fees had already been recovered from the appropriate authority!
Marion thanked the Solicitor for his help and John shook his hand feeling speechless with emotion at his news!
The Solicitor, noticing Marion's ring asked:-
"I see you have an engagement ring Marion!" He said. "Should I be offering my congratulations to you both?"
"Yes! Thank you!" Smiled Marion. "John and I have just become engaged!"
"In that case may I be one of the first to congratulate you both?" He said, shaking both their hands warmly.
After thanking her employer and the rest of her office colleagues, Marion led a rather stunned John outside!
Her boss had insisted Marion should take the rest of the week off and return to work on the following Monday, if she had recovered fully from her experience!
John felt overjoyed with his unexpected news and insisted that they should return home to inform their parents.
As they made their way to the bus stop they heard someone call them!
"Hi Marion!" Said a tall man.
"Hello Julian!" Said Marion throwing her arms round his neck and kissing him.
John was taken aback by this greeting!

"Oh sorry John!" She said quickly. "This is my big Brother Julian."
Julian shook Johns hand and patted him on the back warmly!
"You must be the one I've been hearing so much about!" He said. "You must be a hero if you are taking on my young sister. Only joking John!"
"What are you doing here Ju!" Asked Marion.
"We could not come down earlier, when we heard about you going missing, because we could not get Tim off school and find a child minder." Said Julian. "It took Pauline for ever to get permission from his Headmaster to allow him to come with us today!"
"Where's Pauline now Ju?" Asked Marion, looking around.
"She had to take Tim to the toilet!" Said Julian. "She won't be long! I came to see what time the next bus is. Oh! Here they are now!"
A short pretty blonde woman holding the hand of a young toddler came towards them. Marion went over and kissed the woman and picked up the child.
"Nice to see you Pauline!" Said Marion with a smile. "And how's my favourite Nephew."
John was introduced to the newcomers before they all caught the bus to Marion's house.
John's parents were still there so Marion also introduced them to her Brother and his Wife and son. Marion's parents were of course pleased to see their son, daughter in law and Grandson, although Julian had rung them to say that they were coming down.

During the day David had paid to have the lounge window replaced by the double glazing firm that had initially installed it.
At about 5 o'clock in the afternoon Bulldog arrived to see John.
David suggested John took his friend into the lounge now that it had been tidied up.
Marion said she would join the two of them to leave room for the others to chat in peace in the dining room.
The three of them sat down and John asked Bulldog what happened when the Police arrived after the crashes below Devil's Rock!
"The police arrived about half an hour after you left!" Reported Bulldog. "They examined the wreckage of the two machines, cordoned it off, and sent for an ambulance to pick up the two bodies! Shortly after the police arrived a car with two civilians turned up and started taking photos and measurements of the crash site. We learned later that they were part of a Forensic Team associated with the police. The Police naturally, wanted to know what we were doing there, so Josh's friends said that they had been playing football on the field when the two aircraft flew over and collided above us. Since it was obvious that we could not have been involved in causing the collision, we were free to go. Josh's brother asked one of the policemen if they knew who the victims were. He said they did not know, because there was no identification items on either of the bodies. He did say that the numbers on the Microlight might prove it to be the one that had been reported stolen three months ago from a gliding

club about 150 miles away. The Para-Glider was thought to be a commercially produced type that could have been purchased in kit form from any one of a number of suppliers. The Police were surprised to find that when the paramedics arrived to remove the bodies, they discovered that there was a hand gun and a number of bullets under the body of the man with the Para-Glider! Reporters turned up about three quarters of an hour after the police arrived and took some pictures for the local paper. I managed to have a word with one of them who asked if I had heard about the kidnapping that had been reported in his paper. I said I had read about it and he said he had looked into the case and compiled a list of possible suspects including John. Luckily he did not know that you and I were the ones who rescued Marion John! But he said that although he was pleased that she had been found they still did not know who the kidnapper was. I asked him if he thought the kidnapper was still around! He said he thought it unlikely now that his victim had been found and might be able to identify him. Going back to the crash I told him the police said they did not know who the dead people were! He told me the identity of the two victims would be revealed when their DNA was identified, at which time their names would be published in their paper. I asked him how he would get hold of the DNA results and he told me it would be revealed to the press to enable the police to ask for information from the public in their search for evidence. So John, the police were not concerned with us since there was nothing linking us to the 'accident' anyway. They did mention that the hill was used at

weekends during the summer for parachute and other Aerial sports enthusiasts. But it was rarely used at this time of year and we said the two machines did not come from up there anyway. So no one went up there leaving Josh and his friends, plenty of time to remove any evidence of activity up there."
"Thanks for that Bulldog!" Said John.
"There was something else I wanted to tell you!" Continued Bulldog. "Josh told me about the letter John, that you received from the kidnapper before we rescued Marion. Josh was interested by the man confusing me with someone called 'Gareth' who was supposed to be the son of Sir Arthur Westerfield. I was intrigued by this as well when I heard about it, so I looked up details about it on the Web. It appears that Gareth went missing 18 months ago and there has been no sign of him since. He went missing in the Leeds area of Yorkshire. I could not find a photo of Gareth at first but I did eventually find one in a Leeds paper, published 18 months ago, when he went missing. He did have a slight resemblance to me I suppose, apart from his hair which was shoulder length and curly unlike mine. So what was the kidnappers connection with Gareth? Did he know him before he disappeared, or only after he did? And how did he mistake me for him from an 18 month old photo? Could Gareth have been the kidnappers first victim or is that just a coincidence? Does this mean the kidnapper came from Yorkshire or did he just spend a certain amount of time up there?"
"My brother Julian was up there at University!" Said Marion. "I'll call him!"

She went out and returned with Julian.
John and Bulldog related the details regarding Gareth to Julian.
"Do you remember anything about Gareth, Ju?" Asked Marion.
"I was at Sheffield University and I graduated seven years ago as you know Marion!" Said Julian. "I believe there was a Gareth Westerfield there at about the same time as me, but on a different course. My friend George that I roomed with for the last two years of my degree, once told me about rooming with a posh bloke called Gareth Westerfield during his fresher year. George was on a five year Law course when I knew him, so his fresher year would have been the year before I started my science course."
"Did your friend George tell you anything about Gareth or any of his friends." Asked John.
"I really can't remember!" Said Julian. "After all it would have been 9 years ago that I first roomed with George, and 2 years before that, that he roomed with Gareth! I suppose I could ask George if you think it might be important." Said Julian. "We still keep in touch. And he came to our wedding. I'll give him a bell if you like and you may be able to meet him. He lives and works in London now!"
"Did you remember hearing about Gareth Westerfields disappearance!" Marion asked.
"Not much!" Said Julian. "The name rang a bell at the time, but I never really knew him anyway! And he went missing in Leeds, which I was not familiar with, since I only went there once!"

"I suppose now that the kidnapper is dead!" Said Bulldog thoughtfully. "There's not much point worrying about Gareth anyway! I guess it's just idle curiosity on my part, because I still wonder why the man thought I was Gareth when he shot me!"
"I must say I am also intrigued about that Bulldog!" Said John. "Because that thought that he had, possibly saved my life as he switched his aim from me to you. I'm sorry that you got shot, of course, but you see what I mean!"
"Perhaps that saved my life as well!" Replied Bulldog. "Since he didn't aim properly, and only put a bullet through my shoulder instead of my head!"
"Well I am glad neither of you were killed!" Said Marion, quickly.
"Well it's getting late and I had better get going!" Said Bulldog at last. "I said I would drop in to see Josh and his brother after I came to see you. I want to see how they got on with clearing up on the hill after I left!"
When Bulldog departed, David invited John and his parents to stay for dinner.
Sue had already extended the dining room table and set places for nine now that Julian and his family had arrived!
The mood had improved enormously over the last two days so the meal was a much happier affair.
Everyone was more relaxed than they had been only five or six hours ago.
Marion was still pleased to see her brother and his wife and son.

John spent some time sharing Uni experiences with Julian, who he learned was a Biochemist now, after attaining an Msc in Chemistry at Sheffield!
Julian in turn was interested and surprised at John having not yet obtained a position with his joint Physics and Maths degree.
Marion was pleased to look forward to spending some playtime with her five and a half year old Nephew.
Pauline was of course interested in Marion's wedding plans and asked her how many children she would like!
"I think we want to get properly married before we think about starting a family!" Said Marion with a smile. "This time last year, I was not even thinking of meeting someone, let alone, getting engaged! Do you and Ju want any more children Pauline?"
"Since you asked Marion!" Said Pauline. "I might as well announce that we are expecting an addition to our family in about 6 months time!"
Everyone gathered round Pauline and Julian when they heard Pauline's news.
"Congratulations Pauline and Ju!" Said Marion, hugging them both. "So Tim's going to have a brother or sister soon, and I'll be an auntie again!"
John was pleased to see Marion happy with her family again after the last few weeks. He really liked all of her family now that he had met them.
David went over to John and shook his hand.
"Welcome to our family John!" He said with a smile.
"I hope you haven't been put off now that you have met most of us!"

"How could I when you have been kind enough to allow me to marry your daughter David!" Said John quietly. "I still feel so lucky that she agreed to be my wife!"
"Well don't get too carried away John!" Said Sue with a frown. "When she was a little girl she had a nasty temper if she was annoyed!"
"Thanks for that Mum!" Laughed Marion. "If you put him off he might take my ring back!"
"Thanks for warning me Sue!" Teased John. "I had better make sure I don't annoy her then!"
"You be careful of my mother!" Said Julian, with a wink. "She packs a nasty slap if you rub her up the wrong way! I've still got the bruises to prove it!"
They all laughed and Sue gave John a hug.
"I would like to welcome Marion to our family too!" Said Richard. "Joan and I had almost given up hoping for a Daughter-in-Law!"
"And we could not have asked for a nicer one!" Added Joan giving Marion a hug.
"Thank you both!" Said Marion. "And thank you for having such a perfect son!"
"If we are on the starting line for John and Marion's wedding." Said Julian, with a grin. "Can I put in a bid for Tim as a page boy!"
"Well I can't make a bid for bridesmaid!" Said Pauline patting her tummy. "Are you going to make a bid for Best Man Ju?"
"Enough of that you two!" Laughed David. "You will frighten off the two main contestants!"
"Anyone for a cup of tea?" Said Sue, changing the subject quickly. "I'll go and put the kettle on!"

"I'll come and give you a hand Sue!" Said Joan. "I make it 7 teas and 1 coffee for Richard!"
"I feel really happy for John and Marion!" Sue ventured. "How about you Joan?"
"They make a lovely couple Sue!" Replied Joan. "I have always liked Marion, so I'm glad John has fallen for her too!"
"David was really pleased that John asked his permission to marry Marion Joan!" Said Sue with a grin. "And John was brave to go and face the mad man who kidnapped Marion!"
"I was so proud of him too Sue!" Said Joan. "But that was typical of him! He would do anything for other people and he is very much in love with Marion!"
"I know Joan!" Said Sue. "And I have never seen Marion so happy either!"
"The last few weeks must have been awful for you and David!" Said Joan gently. "I'm glad her kidnapper got killed! And I was pleased that John was the one to rescue Marion with the friend who he calls Bulldog!"
"Yes Joan! That was appropriate I guess!" Said Sue. "And David and I were so glad when John and Bulldog were the ones to bring her home."
"So were Richard and I Sue!" Said Joan. "Now let's take the tea in!"
After all of them had finished drinking their teas and coffee, Pauline took the tired Tim up to bed.
John kissed Marion good night as he and his parents thanked the Ashmores for their hospitality and left for the short walk home.
The rest of the week passed quietly.

Marion and John spent a lot of time together in each other's houses and at the weekend they went to the Multiplex Cinema just outside town to watch a movie. On Sunday John paid for both families to have Sunday Lunch at a nearby Carvery.
Finally Monday arrived and John took Marion to return to her job at the Law firm.
He returned home to wait for Josh, who was at long last coming to have his first reading lesson.
Josh arrived at 11 o'clock carrying the local paper.
"I can't read it!" Said Josh. "But I saw they have a picture of the crash last week. I wondered if they have found out who the two dead ones were yet!"
John took the paper and read the article about the crashes out loud to Josh.
"There's nothing in there about the people that were killed!" Said John. "They might not have got the results of the DNA analysis yet. Anyway Josh let's get you reading shall we?"
"Yes please John!" Said Josh. "I'm looking forward to being at 'school' now. My bro' says he's real pleased I want to go straight now! He's got a job with a delivery company and if he can earn enough money he wants to learn to drive."
"I hope he sticks at it Josh!" Said John. "He's a real bright guy! So is Bulldog! How's he doing after the weekend?"
"He's still going on about that bloke Gareth!" Josh replied. "I don't know why! He keeps on about going up to Leeds's to find out more about the Guy. Oh! And he told me to tell you he's going back to his folks to sort out their differences, whatever that means."

"OK Josh! Let's get started" Said John.
Richard, Johns father was at work and his mother had gone out with Sue Ashmore.
So John and Josh had the house to themselves.
They spent the morning and the rest of the day with John giving Josh reading help.
John sent out for a pizza for lunch for them both, and Josh made good progress.
John found Josh to be an intelligent lad and a quick learner.
At 5 o'clock they packed up and Josh left to go home just before John's mother returned home at 6 o'clock.
"How did your young friend get on?" Asked his mother.
"Pretty well!" John replied. "It amazing how much he remembered from his Primary School. He's very bright actually. Tomorrow we are going to make a start with his writing!"
"We called in at Marion's Law firm!" Said Joan. "As she had finished for the day we brought her home with us!" Said Joan. "She said she would come and see you after she's had something to eat!"
Richard, John's father, arrived home at 7 o'clock with the local evening paper.
"There's a bit in the paper about the crashes out by Devils Rock!" Said Richard. "It seems they do not know the identities of the two victims yet, but from their DNA they do know that they were not related. The gun and ammunition however match their police records to one that was used at a robbery in Yorkshire over five years ago. There is also evidence that the Para-Glider was probably purchased in person from a

Supplier in Sheffield. The Microlight however was stolen a month ago from an enthusiast's landing ground about 150 miles away."
"So we still don't know who the kidnapper was!" Said Joan. "But at least we know he is dead!"
"The Yorkshire connection is interesting dad!" Said John. "I wonder who the woman was though! Maybe she had no connection to the kidnapper at all, since she is assumed by the police to have collided with the Para-Glider. Maybe she saw him crash and just tried to land to help! Of course flying a stolen Microlight doesn't help her case! Does it?"
"Well that will be up to the Police to sort out I suppose!" Concluded Richard. "I wonder if the Ashmore's will hear anything about any suspects in the kidnapping case?"
"Well you can ask Marion Richard!" Said Joan. "She's coming up the path now!"
John went to the door and kissed Marion when she came in.
"How did work go today dear?" He asked.
"It was a bit strange at first!" Replied Marion. "But it was good to get back to normal again! How was your day John?"
"I spent most of the day with Josh!" Said John. "He started his reading lesson at last. He got on pretty well!"
"It's good of you to help him darling!" Said Marion with a smile. "I don't think I have met him yet. Is he related to Bulldog by any chance?"
"No sweetheart!" Said John. "They were two of my friends I met during my Community Service time!"

"I should have known that dearest!" She apologised. "You have spoken about them both many times, but Bulldog is the only one I've met."
"Anyway!" John said. "My father was just telling us what was reported in the local paper about the crash near Devil's Rock! Apparently the police still do not know the identity of the victims!"
"I know!" Said Marion. "My dad bought the same paper!"
"We were wondering if your family had heard anything from the police regarding the kidnapper!" Said John. "Since they don't know he was one of the two people killed!"
"No! We have not heard anything from the police dear" Replied Marion. "But Julian rang his University friend George today to ask him about Gareth. I gather he remembered a few things about him, but I did not have time to talk to Ju before I came to see you John!"
"Never mind darling!" Said John. "It's not that important really! My priorities right now are your happiness and finding myself a job! Now that I have lost my criminal record thanks to your Law colleagues, I can begin looking around for something suitable again!"
"I do love you dear!" Said Marion. "I couldn't wait to get home from work and come and see you tonight. Am I being a silly schoolgirl again?"
"Of course not sweetheart!" Said John, putting his arm round her shoulders. "After the last couple of weeks, I still don't like having to let you out of my sight! Does that make me look like an obsessive idiot as well? I

just want you to get your life back to normal now and spend time with your friends and family."
John realised they were still standing by the open front door so he held her hand and took her to meet his parents!
"What kept you! I thought you were trying to avoid us!" Laughed Joan with a frown. "You're not thinking of eloping are you?"
"No way!" Marion chuckled. "My dad would kill me if we did that. I came over to see my future In-Laws anyway!"
"I like the In-Laws bit Marion!" Said Richard with a smile. "But at the moment it's only an honorary title until you are married!"
"Mum asked me to ask you if you wanted to go out with her tomorrow Mrs Taylor." Asked Marion. "I think she is getting Wedding Fever already."
"Tell her that will be nice Marion! And please call me Joan dear!" Said Joan. "In my eyes your already part of my family!"
"Oh my! You are honoured darling!" Said John quickly "She's my mum but I can't call her Joan!"
They all sat down and Richard got up and put the kettle on and made them tea or coffee while they chatted, happily for the evening!
At half past nine John escorted Marion home and said good night to her and her family before returning to have an early night.

CHAPTER 14 - Julian's Input and the Result

In the morning John once more went to call for Marion to escort her to work.
"You don't need to come with me today dear!" Said Marion. "Although I do like to see you on the way to work, I have to get back to finding my own way like I used to. Also as I told you last night, Ju wants a word with you so come in and I'll see if he's up!"
Julian came down in his dressing gown and they said goodbye to Marion, who left to catch her bus.
Julian took John into the lounge and they sat down. Sue came in with a cup of coffee for Julian and asked John if he preferred tea or coffee? John said he would like a cup of tea if it wasn't too much trouble. Sue brought him his tea and left the two of them to talk.
"I rang my friend George yesterday John!" Began Julian. "To see what he remembered about Gareth Westerfield at Uni and afterwards! He said he had kept in touch with Gareth after they left Sheffield, up to the time that Gareth went missing. George said he was not surprised that Gareth disappeared because he was having a bit of a problem with a chap called Sutherford. Gareth had a girlfriend at the time called Tamzin, who had at one time been engaged to Sutherford. As a result Gareth and Sutherford were clearly not on very good terms. George said, although he was not sure, he thought Sutherford threatened Gareth with violence if he did not break off his relationship with Tamzin. George said he did not know why Tamzin broke off her engagement to Sutherford,

but there were rumours that Sutherford had beaten her up for some reason. George said Gareth continued to have troubles with Sutherford all the time he was at Uni, to such an extent that he failed his degree. As a result Tamzin broke off her relationship with him and went abroad. Apparently this infuriated Sutherford even more and Gareth started getting death threats. Of course he believed they came from Sutherford but that was never proved. So Gareth disappeared about 18 months ago and George has heard nothing from him since then!"

"That's quite a story Julian!" Said John. "Do you think this chap Sutherford could be the man that kidnapped Marion?. If so what had I done to upset him? He couldn't have fancied Marion, I assume, since he kidnapped her and chained her up! So what else made him want to kill me?"

"I have no idea!" Said Julian. "But that incident when Your friend Bulldog got shot does tend to point to someone who knew Gareth."

"I wonder whether your friend George got in touch with Sir Arthur Westerfield, Gareth's dad?" Said John.

"I thought that so I asked him!" Said Julian. "His answer surprised me! He said Sir Arthur was pretty annoyed with George for contacting him! He said George should mind his own business and stop bothering him. George is still upset about the phone call even now. He wondered later if he had been mistaken for someone else who had upset Sir Arthur."

"Could that have been Sutherford?" Said John.

"Yes I suppose it could have been!" Said Julian. "I guess we will never know!"

"Well I'll ask Josh to tell Bulldog about this!" Said John. "Josh is coming round to my place today for some writing lessons!"
"Marion told me about that John!" Said Julian. "It's good of you to do that!"
"Oh I'm sure you would have done the same In the circumstances Julian!" Said John "Anyway! Thanks for the info from George! I had better be going to prepare for Josh's lesson! Thank your mum for the tea and I'll see myself out. Bye!"
John hurried back to his house to wait for Josh.
He knew his mother was going out with Marion's mum, but she had not left yet.
"Did you get Marion to work OK John?" She asked.
"I didn't need to mum!" Replied John. "She took herself today, because she told me Julian wanted to talk to me!"
"Well I expect it will help Marion get back to normal now!" She said. "I'm off now to pick up Sue, dear! Josh will be here in a minute. Won't he? See you later! Bye!"
Josh arrived just before 10 o'clock.
"Am I too early John?" Said Josh. "I got an earlier bus!"
"No Josh it's fine!" Said John at once. "Before we start let me tell you what I learnt from Julian's friend about Gareth!"
John related the information from his meeting with Julian this morning.
"Bulldog will be interested in the info as well Josh!" Said John. "Perhaps you could pass it on to him when you see him!"

"I will if I see him!" Said Josh. "But you might see him before I do! He told me he's going back to his parents place soon, but he was going to come to see you before he left!"
"Well let's get on Josh!" Said John. "I've found a fountain pen for you to use, rather than a ball point! And I have printed out some sheets of paper for you to practice on!"
"Oh yes! Thank you!" Said Josh with a grin. "I remember these writing practice sheets from my time at primary school John!"
Before they could start, the doorbell rang.
John answered it and found Bulldog standing there!
"Hi John!" Said Bulldog. "I am off to my parent's place up in Nottingham. I wanted to see you before I left!"
"Yes I know!" Said John. "Josh has just told me!"
"Sorry!" Said Bulldog quickly. "I forgot Josh was having a lesson today!"
"Never mind!" Said Josh coming to the door. "Come in! We were just talking about something that might interest you!"
Bulldog accepted Josh's invitation and came in.
John related Julian's account of his conversation with George again for Bulldogs benefit.
"That's interesting news!" Said Bulldog. "I had toyed with the idea of ringing Sir Arthur Westerfield myself, but I was not sure if he would want to talk to me about Gareth!"
"Did you have his number then Bulldog?" Asked Josh.

"Yes I looked it up on Directory Inquiries! I was surprised that it was not an ex-directory number!" Said Bulldog.
"Well ring him now!" Said Josh with a grin.
"Yes you can use our phone Bulldog!" Said John. "I am interested anyway, to see what happens if you get through to him!"
"Well it's your phone John!" Said Bulldog. "So you ring! I'll give you his number!"
"No Bulldog!" Said John at once. "You were the one that was shot and mistaken for Gareth! So you ring!"
Bulldog took out the number and handed it to John who dialled it before handing the phone to Bulldog.
"I've put the phone on speakerphone so we can all hear!" Said John. "Keep quiet!"
They could hear the phone ringing and then heard someone answer it.
"Hello! This is Sir Arthur Westerfields, Secretary! Can I help you!" A female voice said.
"Can I speak to Sir Arthur please?" Said Bulldog.
"Who shall I tell him is calling?" She said.
"My name is Walter Handley. He will not know me but I have been asked to give him some information." Said Bulldog politely.
"You can give me the information, and I will pass it on to Sir Arthur." She said
"That's good of you, but I was told only to speak to Sir Arthur." Said Bulldog, politely once more.
"Hold on! I'll see if he wishes to talk to you!" She said
The phone went silent for about a minute.
"Sir Arthur will take your call! I'll put you through!" She said.

After a short pause a man's voice was heard.
"Arthur Westerfield here! Can I help you?" He said.
"My name is Walter Handley Sir Arthur!" Said Bulldog politely "You don't know me I'm afraid, but I was shot by someone who mistook me for your son Gareth. I realise I should not be ringing you with this information, but I was worried that the person could be after your son."
"Do you know who shot you?" Queried Sir Arthur.
"Not his name I'm afraid!" Said Bulldog. "But I have information that he was killed in an accident a week ago. I don't know if he has any accomplices so I wanted to warn you!"
"Thank you Walter!" Said Sir Arthur. "You may not know that my son Gareth, went missing 18 months ago."
"No! I didn't know that!" Lied Bulldog. "I'm sorry if I have offended or upset you by ringing you!"
"That's not a problem!" Replied Sir Arthur gently. "Thank you for letting me know about being mistaken for Gareth. Please tell me about what caused you to get shot!"
Bulldog told him about Marion being kidnapped and the kidnapper victimising John! Ending finally with details of his crash and subsequent death. He said the police had not so far identified the man or woman that had been killed.
"I think I know who might have mistaken you for Gareth!" Said Sir Arthur. "And possibly the woman. But unless I'm sure I prefer not to name them! However my Secretary will have your phone number, so if I can get down to your area, I will make some

inquiries and I would then like to come and visit you. My Secretary has taken down the information you gave me, so thank you for that now and I hope to meet you later. Goodbye!"

Said Bulldog as he put down the phone. "But he seemed pleased I phoned him anyway!"
"So you still don't know who the dead people are!" Said Josh.
"No!" Said Bulldog. "But we may learn something if he comes down to see us!"
"Just a couple of things though!" Said Josh carefully. "Firstly he has Johns phone number. And secondly he thinks Walter Handley lives here not John!"
"Yes! You are right Josh!" Said John. "It could be a problem if my parents take the call! Anyway at least he didn't refuse to talk to you like he did when Julian's friend George phoned him!"
"Are you still going back to your parents place Bulldog?" Asked Josh.
"Yes I am Josh!" Replied Bulldog. "But I guess I ought to wait for a couple of days to see if Sir Arthur rings up or comes down!"
"In the mean time let's get you doing a bit of writing Josh!" Said John quietly. "You are welcome to stay Bulldog! If you like I'll put a film on for you and order a take away for lunch!"
Bulldog accepted John's invitation and sat down with a video, while Josh practised his writing under John's tutelage! Josh got on well again during the day and took some sheets home to practice on. John told him to come back in the morning to carry on with his lessons.

Bulldog gave John his mobile number and asked him to call him if Sir Arthur rings him.
Josh and Bulldog left together just before 5 o'clock and John took the opportunity to catch a bus and go to meet Marion from work.
"This is a nice surprise darling!" Said Marion, kissing him. "How did you get on with Ju?"
John told her about all that had happened during the day as they drove home on the bus.
When they got to Marion's house they found Joan, Johns mother there.
"Sue has asked us to stay for dinner John!" Said Joan. "Pauline and Julian took Tim out to London for the day. They are on the train now and when they get to town they are going to fetch in some fish and chips for everyone if that's OK!" I've rung your dad John so he will come here instead of going home!"
"Julian told me to tell you he wants to see you when he gets back John!" Said Sue. "Sorry its only fish and chips but Joan and I have been out all day!"
"That will be fine!" Said John and Marion.
Richard and David arrived together, about half an hour before Pauline and Julian carried in a tired Tim.
Pauline took Tim up to bed before coming down to help Sue and Joan serve up the fish and chips.
"There's salt and vinegar on the table!" Said Pauline. "The ladies are doing some bread and butter. Can someone dish out the knives and forks?"
"I'll do that!" Said Marion. "Are there enough plates and glasses to go round Pauline? If not there are some more in the dishwasher!"

"I'll pour out the drinks!" Said Julian."Can you give me a hand John?"
"I think we have enough plates and glasses Marion!" Said Pauline. "Everyone sit down and I'll fetch the things in!"
Finally everything was ready and they all enjoyed their makeshift dinner, after which the four ladies cleared up the dinner things while the gentlemen retired to the lounge.
"That was nice!" Said John, feeling pleasantly full.
"I've always liked a bit of fish and chips!"
"Yes!" Added Julian. "It takes a bit of beating! Doesn't it?"
The Ladies came in to join their other halves and Sue asked who wanted coffee!
Pauline said she would make the coffee and Marion said she would help her so the two mothers, Sue And Joan, could sit down and relax.
After their coffee they all sat back to unwind or discuss their days out.
Marion snuggled up with John while he told Julian about the conversation Bulldog had with Sir Arthur Westerfield this morning. He said because Sir Arthur had refused to name names they had not learnt anything new!.
Thus they all had a pleasant and relaxing evening together, before Julian and Pauline retired at about half past nine, to their bedroom after a tiring day with Tim in London.
John and his parents left at ten thirty after thanking David and Sue for their hospitality.

John kissed Marion good night as they left and reflected on the events of the day, as he walked home, thinking it had been an interesting experience.
Later he lay in bed wondering if he was any nearer to finding out who the man and woman were that had caused him and Marion so much grief!

CHAPTER 15 - Another Piece of the Puzzle and a Problem

The following morning John was late waking up. This was partly because his parents had both gone out early, and his mother had decided to let him lie in rather than rousing him.

He realised, with regret, it was too late to go and see Marion before she went off to work, so he lay in his bed contemplating what he should do today apart from Josh's lessons.

He also realised it was only a week ago that he had been up on Devil's Rock, facing the kidnapper.

The thought of the encounter and demise of his attacker still made him shudder and he still could not get his head round the reason for him being victimised by the man.

There seemed to be no sense or motive in the treatment he received from his opponent. Why was Marion kidnapped on the day he had met her after finishing his Community Service?

At that time they were barely friends not a couple. Her parents received the ransom notes, so why was he told to go to Blake's Mill and Devil's Rock rather than one of them?.

It didn't make sense!

Was he being stalked perhaps?

If so that would mean his stalker would have to be either a woman or perhaps a 'gay' man, because straight men do not normally stalk straight men!

Therefore, since he had been contacted by phone and the voice certainly sounded male, it would mean his opponent would have to be gay if he was a stalker!
So why did he try to shoot me and get Bulldog instead?
If on the other hand he was being stalked by a woman it could explain why Marion was kidnapped and it could have been a women shooting at him and riding the motorbike. But the person on the Para-Glider was certainly male as confirmed by the police after he died.
The only other woman that he thought might be involved was the pilot of the Microlight. And there is no real evidence that she was involved with the Para-glider chap, since, unknown to the police, she did not collide with the Para-Glider.
Of course there was one other possible stalker.
That was Marion!
Could she be considered?
If so she would have had to only pretend to be kidnapped.
This was extremely unlikely because she was certainly chained up when he and Bulldog found her in the underground room at Blake's Mill.
And since she could not have known that they were going to go there she would have had to chain herself up and bolt the door on the outside as well.
Or need an accomplice to do it, which would be unreasonable, unless they were there all the time in case someone came along unexpectedly.
No! He was sure Marion could not have had anything to do with his victimisation, and he started to wonder

if he was becoming paranoid to have even thought she could behave like that!
So what was he left with?
The man on the Para-Glider, the Microlight pilot, an unknown stalker or someone else that had a grudge against him for some reason.
He could not think of anyone he might have inadvertently upset at any time.
He could not therefore make any sense of anything that had happened, so he got up, dressed and had some breakfast while he waited for Josh.
He noticed it had started raining and an hour later a rather damp Josh arrived with another copy of the local paper.
"Hi Josh!" Said John as he opened the front door. "I see its raining again! Is there anything new in the paper today?"
"I have been trying out my reading!" Smiled Josh. "I didn't get past the headlines though before it rained. There has been another fight at our local footie ground again. And more binge drinking arrests by our plods. Just the usual things! I think there is a bit more inside about the crash, but it was becoming a bit hard for me to read. It's still a bit damp! You have a look!"
John took Josh's paper and thumbed through it.
The bit about the crash was on the bottom of page 4.
He read it and told Josh what it said
"It still says they do not know who the dead people were!" Said John. "They are going to be circulating artists portraits of the victims hoping someone will recognise them.

The police said their details do not match with anyone on their missing persons lists. There was no identifiable store labels or anything else in either of their clothes. Not much new there Josh!"
"I thought they ought to know who they were by now!" Said Josh.
"Hang on a minute!" Said John. "This bit at the bottom is interesting! It appears the bullets found in the gun and on the man were blanks. Why should that be?"
"It means he was not trying to kill you John!" Said Josh. "So why was he shooting at you? Was he hoping to scare you into jumping off Devil's Rock?"
"Well he wasn't using blanks when he shot Bulldog Josh!" Said John. "I don't get it! It doesn't make sense!"
"It's all a bit weird!" Said a puzzled Josh.
"I've just read something else here as well!" Said John. "It says here that when they examined the Para-Glider they found all the cords attached to the oblong parachute had been cut through just enough to weaken them."
"Oh! That's a bit worrying!" Said Josh. "I hope they don't find out that me and Bulldog did that!"
"You told me you only weakened one of them didn't you?" Said John.
"Yes that's right John!" Said Josh.
"Well this report says they were all weakened Josh!" Said John. "So who tampered with the other three? And why?"
"Well it certainly wasn't me and Bulldog!" Said Josh fervently. "It took us some time to do one, and we

were worried someone would come and disturb us! Give Bulldog a ring and he'll tell you the same!"
"I wasn't doubting you Josh!" Said John quickly. "I was just wondering when the cords were tampered with? I imagine you would have known if they had been interfered with when you sabotaged one of them. That would mean they were tampered with after you left. It also meant that someone must have had a key to the padlock! I presume you locked it again when you and Bulldog left."
"Yes we did!" Said Josh. "So someone must have been there after we left on Sunday morning but before he took off on Monday lunchtime."
"So someone else wanted to injure or kill the person flying the Para-Glider!" Said John. "And the person flying it on Monday only had blanks in his gun!"
"Maybe whoever sabotaged the Para-Glider also changed the bullets in the gun to blanks as well!" Said Josh.
"Why do you think they would do that?" Said John. "Could it mean the person flying the machine was not the kidnapper? In which case he or she must still be around."
"That's a worrying thought!" Said Josh. "It would mean you could be still in danger John!"
"Not only me but Marion and her family as well!" Said John. "I suppose I had better get the police involved now! I'll give them a ring now! Sorry about your lesson Josh! We'll have to do it later!"
"Of course!" Said Josh quickly. "I had better go and warn Bulldog as well John!"
Josh packed up his things and left.

John phoned the Police Station and asked to speak to someone regarding either the crash or the kidnap of Marion!
He was asked a couple of questions and invited to call in person at the Police Station as soon as possible, so John put on his shirt, tie and suit, grabbed his coat and walked to the bus stop.
Although the rain shower had eased off, the bus still seemed to take forever to get to town, so when it arrived John made straight for the Police Station.
He recognised the Sergeant at the desk from his last visit but neither of them mentioned it and John gave him his name and asked to see the person that he spoke to on the phone.
He was shown into an office on the first floor.
A man in plain clothes, introduced himself as DC Tony Matthews, and asked John to sit down and explain what he was concerned about.
Of course John found the man already knew about Bulldogs shooting and the rescue of Marion.
He did not know however about the intended meeting at Devil's Rock with the supposed kidnapper.
John told him about the phone call and the man taking a shot at Marion as a warning if he did not go to Devil's Rock.
John said there was no way he was going up there, but Walter Handley, also known as Bulldog, wanted to go in John's place after being previously been shot by the man.
John told the policeman that since he was not going up there his friends suggested they would stay hidden at

the bottom of the path, which was the only way up to the top of the hill, to intercept anyone that arrived!
It turned out to be unnecessary in the end because they found the man arrived on a Para-Glider instead of on foot.
They heard the machine arrive on the hill and circle round with the man looking down. He must have spotted one of them because he started shooting before climbing higher. As he tried to turn a Microlight appeared.
They heard a snapping sound and saw the Oblong parachute on the machine begin to deflate.
They assumed the Para-Glider had collided with the Microlight, although they were too far away to be certain.
They did however see the Para-Glider fall spinning out of the sky and crash.
The Microlight followed it down and eventually also crashed.
They ran over to the crashed machines but it was too late to save either of the victims. John said he and they assumed that the dead man was the kidnapper, but had no idea who the pilot of the Microlight was.
Seeing the report in the local paper left a doubt in John's mind, when he read about the Para-Glider being sabotaged by someone, and the gun being loaded with blanks.
He said he was afraid this might mean the person who died may not have been the kidnapper and he could therefore still be around and dangerous, since he had already demonstrated that he had and used a rifle.

The policeman listened to Johns story and after asking a few questions called for one of his Superiors, who came to see John.
Having listened to John and checked some of the facts with the detective responsible for handling the investigation of the crash victims, the Senior Officer thanked John for his summary of the situation and his concern regarding the kidnapper.
He was also interested about the kidnappers reference in his letter, which John produced for him to read, to Bulldog resembling Gareth Westerfield.
John told him they had contacted Sir Arthur Westerfield to see if he knew who might have known his son.
The officer asked one of the detectives to contact Sir Arthur and arrange transport if he was willing to come down and help with their enquiries.
John said he was now concerned for the safety of his and Marion's families if the kidnapper was still out there!
The Officer agreed there would be difficulties apprehending the suspect, because no one appeared to have any idea of his appearance origin or identity.
"If you are right about Sir Arthur!" He said. "He may have some idea of the identity of the suspect, but for the present we will need to provide protection for you and your families. It would simplify our job if you could all congregate in one place for the time being. I will then assign a firearms officer to safeguard you all. Where are all your family members now?"
"Marion and my fathers are at work!" Said John. "Our mothers were going out together today, but I don't

know where! Marion's Brother and his wife and son were again going out but I don't know where. Marion works at the Law firm in the high street so I will need to go and collect her!"
"Do your parents have mobile phones?" Said the Officer. "If so can you contact them and tell them to return home? The same applies to Marion's Brother. I will provide you with an unmarked car and driver, to avoid attracting attention, to take you and Marion home!"
"Can I contact Bulldog, whose real name is Walter Handley, and get him to warn his friends to keep undercover!" Asked John.
"Of course if you have his number!" Said the Officer. "I will contact you if and when Sir Arthur arrives. I would like you both here if he has any idea about the suspect or the identity of either of the deceased from the crashes! I hear your car is outside and ready now to take you and Marion home!"
John had suggested that they should all congregate at Marion's house, because it was larger than his own! John asked the driver of the car to stop outside the Law firm where Marion worked, while he went and fetched her.
He went in and asked for her and when she came, he told her what was happening.
She informed her boss of the arrangement, collected her coat and bag and returned with John to the car. When they got to her house they found their parents had already arrived. Marion's Brother, Julian and his wife and son however, had not come home yet.

There were 2 plain clothed men and 4 police firearms officers there already.
They were inspecting the house and grounds to decide how many personnel were required and where to position them.
John was relieved to have Marion with him now!
They were told Sue had already been informed that John and his family would be staying at her house for the foreseeable future!
So she had set up a spare camping bed in Marion's room for John and two more for Richard and Joan in the dining room.
One of the plain clothed policemen said they should let him know if they required anything brought in, so he could organise the delivery.
No one was to leave the house for any reason unless they were accompanied by a firearms officer.
When Julian and his family arrived, Sue and Joan had cooked a meal for them all!
They all then needed to prepare for what could be a long wait!
John was happy to be sleeping in Marion's room, because he wanted to be near her if anything happened during the night!
David provided John and Richard with pyjamas, dressing gowns and slippers!
Sue did the same for Joan!
Marion was pleased to have John with her at night, but worried that she might snore or talk in her sleep or something, which might give John a bad impression of his future wife!

Richard and Joan would rather be sleeping in their own bed in their own house, but accepted the temporary arrangement with a certain amount of resignation since they saw no other option, in present circumstances!
Julian would have liked to be able to move his family back to Peterborough but was also resigned to the present arrangement!
Pauline, on the other hand, was worried about Tim missing school!
David and Sue were least worried by the arrangement, since they enjoyed having a house full of guests, although David, like Richard, was a bit worried about being off work for any length of time!
The plain clothed policeman ensured that Richard and David's phone numbers were reallocated to the police station to ensure any calls would be intercepted.
The night passed without incident and Sue and Joan woke early and prepared breakfast for everyone including the police officers who had been outside during the night.
The firearms officer had spent part of the night with night-vision glasses looking for likely places that the kidnapper might have been at when he fired the shot that broke the window and vase when Marion was seated in the lounge.
He identified three possible locations that could have been used!
He contacted the police station and asked for someone from the traffic division to check them out.
The firearms officer was relieved by one of his colleagues at 9 o'clock and the plain clothes officer

returned to the station to see if any calls had been received.
He returned at mid day to inform John that Sir Arthur would be coming down the following day.
John had a call on his mobile phone from Bulldog to see if everyone was OK!
Bulldog said he had spent the night with Josh's family without incident.
He also confirmed that the Para-Gliders cords were all intact when Josh and him were trying to sabotage the parachute.
John told him to stay indoors and take care!
There was nothing for everyone in the house to do apart from watching television or reading so life became rather boring.
Pauline let Tim watch children's TV to keep him amused and Marion and John played games with him for the same purpose.
The police advised them to keep the curtains drawn in the lounge and David and Sues bedroom because they had windows at the front of the house.
The police also set up bulletproof screens in those two rooms in case they were shot at!
After another night without incident a car arrived to take John to the police station to meet with Sir Arthur.
After an uneventful journey to the Police Station John was taken to a conference room on the second floor.
The room was furnished with a large table surrounded by chairs.
The uniformed Senior Officer that he had met on his previous visit was sitting at one end of the table

flanked by several plain clothed officers some of whom John had also met.
He was offered a chair at one side of the table and shortly after his arrival another door was opened and Sir Arthur was escorted into the room by another uniformed officer.
Sir Arthur Westerfield was a medium height, balding, grey haired man, looking to John to be a few years older than his father Richard.
He was dressed as John would have expected in a smart grey business suit with a white shirt and tie.
He had obviously already met the Police officers so John was introduced to him as he sat down opposite him at the table.
"Good morning John!" Said Sir Arthur affably. "I was expecting to meet Walter Handley, who spoke to me a few days ago."
John explained that the phone call had been made by Walter, alias Bulldog, from his land line because he was visiting John at that time!
" I'm sorry for any confusion Sir Arthur!" John said. "Walter replaced the receiver before I had time to introduce myself!"
"Hence the confusion!" Sir Arthur said. "And please drop the Sir and call me Arthur!"
The Senior Officer then outlined the background to the situation that they were now experiencing.
He passed round pictures of the crash site and details of the victims which he said were now residing in the local Mortuary.
He asked John to sum up his experiences regarding the kidnap and rescue of Marion.

John did so mentioning being told to go to Blake's Mill which resulted in Bulldog being shot and seeing someone that he assumed to be the kidnapper, depart on a motorcycle. He then related the letter he received which contained a lock of Marion's hair, and which mentioned Bulldogs similarity to Gareth, Sir Arthur's son.

The letter had also told him to go to Devil's Rock. John went on to relate the rescue of Marion by himself and Bulldog followed by the phone call from the kidnapper which resulted in the shooting of the window of Marion's lounge.

The various events were confirmed by the Senior Officer.

Sir Arthur was asked if he had any idea of the possible identities and/or the motive regarding the kidnapping or shooting plus the identities of the deceased from the crashes.

"Firstly I must tell you that my son did not disappear as it has been reported!" Said Sir Arthur quietly. "As the Police know, I was advised by the Police Force in Leeds to announce Gareth's disappearance to the papers because he had received a number of death threats. Gareth therefore changed his name and moved to the USA where he met up with his former girl friend Tamzin Outhwait to whom he is now married!"

"So do you know who was threatening Gareth?" Asked John. "If so do you have any idea what happened to him or her?"

"I notice you say him or her!" Said Sir Arthur quickly. "Does that mean you think there is a chance that the person who kidnapped Marion was a woman?"

"I don't know!" Said John. "But I have just tried to look at all possibilities recently!"
"Well I am pretty certain Gareth's tormentor was male!" Said Sir Arthur. "The Police tended also to agree with me, but because of lack of conclusive evidence they could not intervene at that time, hence the suggestion that Gareth should disappear!"
"I accept that!" Interrupted the Senior Officer. "But unofficially, who was the main suspect?"
"I believe it was a fellow student at Gareth's University!" Sir Arthur replied. "His name is Vincent Sutherford. He and Gareth were at secondary school together before both obtaining places on the same History course at Sheffield University. Tamzin Outhwait was at the same primary school as Gareth, but when he got to Sheffield be found that she was engaged to Vincent. This did not upset Gareth and he and Vincent remained friends at first. However for some reason Tamzin and Vincent's relationship broke down and she broke off their engagement. I don't know the details, but it was rumoured that they had a huge row and Vincent beat her up. Tamzin turned to Vincent's friend Gareth for support and they eventually became good friends. Their relationship clearly upset Vincent, who unfairly blamed Gareth for turning Tamzin against him even though at that time Tamzin was not Gareth's girlfriend. Vincent began to make threats against Gareth, which Gareth ignored at first. Tamzin left University and took a job overseas to get away from Vincent and to relieve as she felt tensions between Gareth and Vincent. Unfortunately her leaving had the opposite effect, because Vincent

believed Gareth had persuaded her to go away in order to annoy him! The situation was not helped because Gareth was seen around with another female student called Morrison. I do not know her Christian name because there was never any relationship between them. Vincent however believed there was, so the threats continued. Finally in their final year the relationship between them deteriated to such an extent that both of them failed their finals. It was too much for Gareth to bear so he did not bother to resit his degree final, although Vincent did do so and passed. I think Gareth believed the bad feeling between them would cease once he left University, but that did not happen. He now began to receive death threats and it began to take its toll after a couple of years. I contacted the police on his behalf and as I have said eventually they recommended Gareth should disappear. Tamzin had kept in touch with Gareth and she contacted him and he went out to meet her in Chicago. They are now married and both have gained a place at University in Boston. Vincent was left with no one to take out his venom on so he moved away. I have no idea where he went so he could have come here, but why he should have taken a dislike to you John, if it is him, I can't understand."
"Do we know what this Vincent looks like Sir Arthur?" Asked the Senior Officer.
"I knew him when they were both at school, but I only met him once at Uni during Gareth's fresher year." Replied Sir Arthur. "I would say he is shorter than John. I would estimate him to be about 5 foot 4 inch tall slim build dark hair. I believe the Leeds police sent

you a photo that they obtained from his ID card at Uni."
"Yes that's correct." Said the Senior Officer. "It confirms he was not the person killed on the Para-Glider anyway! So we still do not know who either of the dead persons were! We have of course issued the photo to our people to enable them to keep a lookout in this area!"
John was also given a photo of Vincent to see if any of his or Marion's family recognised him.
The Senior Officer then wound up the meeting and thanked everyone for their contributions!
John was then driven back again to Marion's house and Marion was pleased to have John back with her!
The rest of them at the Ashmore's residence, had endured another boring but otherwise thankfully uneventful day!
Sue and Joan had amused themselves by making some cookies and muffins!
At the same time, Tim had been allowed to make a couple of gingerbread men which he decorated once they were cool!
The plain-clothes constable brought in the morning papers so at least, they had something to read!
They all gathered in the lounge now, to hear how John had got on at the Police Station with Sir Arthur Westerfield!
John related the information regarding Gareth and Vincent and showed them the photo of Vincent in his student days!
No one, including even Julian, who may have seen him at Uni, recognised Vincent from the photo, which

was hardly surprising since no one, including Marion who had been kidnapped, had seen him!
John said that the person riding the motorbike was most likely Vincent because he had been quite small!
"So Sir Arthur could not think of anything that might account for Vincent kidnapping Marion or victimising John!" Said Julian. "Therefore we are no nearer to discovering any motive for his actions!"
"I vaguely remember Gareth Westerfield, way back when I first went to Sheffield!" Said Pauline suddenly. "That was before I met Ju! I was not involved with him at all, but I think I may have been visiting a girl friend of mine who lived in the same Hall of Residence as Gareth. I think I was probably talking to Gareth in the kitchen while my friend was doing her washing when this small guy came in and started having a go at Gareth. It was a long time ago! I seem to remember telling the small guy to cool it! But that might have been my friend who said that! I think I may have seen Gareth a few times to pass the time of day like I would with any other student. The photo of Vincent did not ring any bells either, but he might have been the small man I suppose!"
"I didn't realise you and Julian met at Uni Pauline!" Said John thoughtfully.
"What was your maiden name?"
"That's easy!" Said Marion quickly. "Its Morrison isn't it Pauline? Why do you want to know John?"
"Because Sir Arthur mentioned that he understood this guy Vincent thought Gareth had a girlfriend called Morrison. He couldn't remember her first name so I did not connect it to you." Replied John.

"Well I was never a girlfriend of Gareth!" Said Pauline indignantly. "In fact I hardly knew him really!"
"Even so!" Said Julian slowly. "This Vincent must have thought you were dear! It might be why he came down here when he thought Gareth disappeared! Maybe he thought you had married Gareth, and he had changed his name for some reason or other!"
"That's preposterous!" Said Pauline. "He would have had to be pretty stupid to think that! Wouldn't he! After all we live in Peterborough anyway, not here!"
"I think his obsession with Gareth does point to the fact that he was rather unstable!" Said John quickly. "But it still doesn't explain why I was a target for his actions!"
"If he has a mental problem you might have been someone in the wrong place at the right time, or vice versa!" Said Julian. "Maybe you meeting Marion that evening triggered something in his warped mind that reminded him of Gareth with Tamzin! perhaps that was why, on the spur of the moment, he seized Marion as a means of getting at you! I realise that sounds pretty stupid, but I have heard of things like this happening!"
"It's a good theory!" Said John! "But it still doesn't explain why he managed to persuade someone to take his place on a sabotaged Para-Glider armed only with a gun loaded with blanks."
"It just might if he suddenly realised he was targeting the wrong man and he wanted to find a way of getting away!" Said Julian. "He possibly hoped the person on the machine would be forced to land, get arrested and identified as the kidnapper, allowing him to get away

in the confusion! Of course it all went wrong when the impostor crashed, but even that was in his favour because the dead man could not answer any awkward questions! Even the appearance of the woman on the Microlight may have added to the deception, by getting herself killed! Everyone, including ourselves and the Police, believed she was connected to the kidnapper! Even the fact that she was flying a stolen Microlight probably added to that conclusion too!"
"So you reckon the man has probably left this area now and gone back to wherever he came from?" Said Marion. "In which case, we wouldn't need to hide like this any longer?"
"Yes! That may be true!" Said John. "But we don't know for certain, if Julian's supposition is correct of course. We will need to discuss the possibility with the police, before they decide whether we can relax again!"
"Well let's hope it is right!" Said David. "But it will still mean the only way to prove it is the need to apprehend Vincent, or whoever is the kidnapper! So let's hope the police can manage that!"
"If not we will be stuck here indefinitely!" Said Richard wearily.
"Excuse me for a moment!" Said John. "I'll just go and change into something more comfortable!"
"You will find a suitcase up there!" Said Richard. "I got permission to go home to collect a few things while you were away!"
"Thanks dad!" Said John. "I won't be a minute!"
"I'll come with you and help you put your clothes away!" Said Marion.

"Thanks dear!" Said John.
John and Marion went up to her bedroom and John unpacked his suitcase, while Marion found space in her cupboards for his clothes!
John glanced out of the bedroom window and saw there was now a new prefabricated shed on the garden lawn.
"What's that Marion?" He asked.
"It's the Police's temporary control room John!" Said Marion. "They got some chaps to put it up while you were out dear! It means they can keep in touch with their Station, and have somewhere to sleep while they are off duty! I had a look at it when they set it up and found its quite comfortable inside, with a bed, chairs and a desk etc!"
"Well it keeps them out of the rain I guess!" Said John. "I noticed the rain had almost stopped when I came home! I suppose someone ought to go and have a chat with whoever is in charge down there, to see if there have been any further developments!"
"Let's just have a quiet time together first John!" Said Marion, giving him a hug. "Can I just be a silly schoolgirl again, and enjoy being with my future husband for a few moments!"
"I like the sound of that dear!" Smiled John as he kissed her. "I just need a quick wash, and when I've changed, let's go and join the others and find a seat together somewhere."
They went down hand in hand and Sue suggested they went and sat in the lounge to relax before dinner.

Pauline had volunteered to cook their evening meal and the two mothers had said they would kelp with the preparation.
Tim was upstairs with Julian now, doing some school work, because Pauline was worried about him missing too much time off from his school.
She had informed Tim's school about their enforced necessity of being unable to return home!
Tim's teacher had suggested things to give Tim to do, and agreed to send some things by post for them to help him with!
David and Richard were not good at doing nothing, so they had got out some of the board games that David found plus playing cards etc.
They were sitting in the lounge when John and Marion went in, engaged in a game of chess.
"It's been a while since I played this!" Said Richard. "I had forgotten the moves!"
"Same here!" Replied David. "The last time I played was with Julian before he went to Uni! You never liked chess did you Marion?"
"No Dad!" Marion replied. " Ju tried to teach me when we were younger, but I never got the hang of it! How about you John?"
"I used to play a bit at Uni, but a few of us used to play Monopoly or cards!" Said John.
"What did you play at cards?" Asked David.
"Some of us played Bridge!" Replied John. "But I was never too keen on it! So I preferred Black Maria or Brag. We never had enough money to play Poker or Pontoon."

"I was never bright enough to go to University!" Said Marion.
"I can't accept that Marion!" Said David quickly. "You were top of the class at school, but you and your friend Betty Kingsnorth wanted to go to the local College and do Business Studies! That's why you are now a good Legal Secretary and isn't Betty a Medical Secretary at our local Hospital?"
"Alright you win Dad!" Said Marion. "Neither of us decided to follow her brother or Julian and go to University, so we skipped sixth form and went to College for a couple of years instead! I still enjoy my job and I know that Betty did as well before she got married. She now has two daughters!"
"That reminds me Marion!" Said John seriously. "I've never met any of your friends! Have I?"
"The same applies to me John!" Said Marion. "I've only met Bulldog and Josh, who were your Community Service buddies. I don't know any of your other
friends either!"
"Well neither of you will meet anyone if we don't get out of this soon!" Said David.
"Well at least we have each other now dear!" Said John placing his arm round Marion's shoulders.
"Yes John we do!" Said Marion with her head on his shoulder. "And I can never be happier than I am now!"
"Oh it takes you back to your courting days! Doesn't it David?" Laughed Richard.
"I can't remember that far back!" Smiled David.
They were interrupted by someone knocking on the back door.

They heard Sue go and open it and she came into the lounge followed by one of the plain clothed Officers.

CHAPTER 16 - Solutions at Last.

"I've just received word that Vincent Sutherford was seen yesterday morning near his mother's house in Blackley, a suburb of Manchester!" Said the Officer. "He was found to be armed with a hand gun and rifle! Realising he had been spotted, he took cover in an empty house from where, being cornered, he fired several shots at one of our constables, before being shot in the arm and leg by a Firearms Officer! Having been injured he was forced to surrender, arrested and taken to hospital in order to have his injuries treated! He has since been interviewed by the local Constabulary and is now under police guard in the hospital! Once he is discharged, he will be transferred to the local prison hospital wing to await his trial! I have also just been informed that today he has confessed to the kidnap of Miss Ashmore, plus the Vendetta with Mr John Taylor! I don't have any further details at the moment but hopefully it should mean your safety should now no longer be a problem! I am waiting for further confirmation from my Superiors before disbanding our protection team. I'll keep you informed!"

"That sounds good!" Said Richard with a sigh of relief. "Let's hope we can begin to get back to normality again!"

"I feel a lot happier now Vincent has been caught!" Said John. "But I would still like to know why I became his target! Perhaps I will never know now!"

"I am glad you are out of danger too, dear!" Said Marion kissing him. "I hope we can never experience events like we have recently again!"

The following morning the Senior Officer in charge of the case came to the Ashmore's house, just before lunch, to inform them about the present situation regarding Vincent Sutherford.

"The accused has now made a full confession!" Said the Officer.

Here is a transcript that I have just received today from my Colleague's in the

Manchester Police Force! He read:-

He claims his actions were instigated by a pathological hatred of Gareth Westerfield for a variety of reasons. When the object of his hatred disappeared his loathing was transferred towards the person he associated with being the female companion of Gareth. This person he believed had the surname of Morrison. He believed this Morrison female married someone called Ashmore after Gareth disappeared.

He also knew there was a Julian Ashmore at Sheffield at the same time as himself and Gareth. He made inquiries and found there was a Marion Ashmore living at the address which the Ashmore at University was registered at. He therefore assumed that Marion Ashmore was the married name of Marion Morrison, and therefore the former girlfriend of Gareth. When he looked on the electoral roll for this address there was no Julian Ashmore registered here only Marion Ashmore. He then made yet another assumption by believing Marion Ashmore (nee Morrison) was divorced from Julian Ashmore. He arrived outside this address one evening just as Marion was meeting John Taylor. His warped mind imagined John Taylor was a colleague of Gareth and that he was acting as a go between for Marion and Gareth. So he took the opportunity to kidnap Marion, hoping to use her to flush out Gareth. When nothing happened after a couple of days he decided to try and get hold of John Taylor. That's why he tried to lure John to Drakes Mill. This misfired when John turned up with Walter Handley (who John knew as Bulldog). He thought Walter was Gareth and shot him. He thought he had killed him, so he left the scene and rode off on his motor cycle. When he learnt later that it wasn't Gareth that he shot (and he had not killed Walter), he turned his attention back to John again, to try to get IBM global to reveal the whereabouts of Gareth. It is not clear, in his mind, why he decided to try and get John to go up to Devil's Rock , and the events it led to are therefore rather confused. More so because two people died as a result of it.

He has however revealed that he knew both of the people that died, but he has not yet agreed to identify them.

"That's as much as we have been able to reveal at present!" Said the Senior Officer. "Vincent is being assessed by a local psychiatrist! He will be interviewed again later today! Hopefully he will cooperate fully and reveal more details! I or one of my team will inform you of any developments. I will be communicating with Sir Arthur Westerfield later today to update him on recent events! In the meantime I am standing my protection team down now that it is safe for you to return your lives to normality. Thank you for your assistance!"

The police team left with their Senior Officer after making arrangements to remove all of the items installed at the Ashmore's premises!

Sue and Joan served up a quick meal for everyone when the police left

"Well I'm glad that's over!" Said Richard with feeling. "Not the lunch! I didn't mean that! I mean the business with that Vincent creature! Anyway I'm off home to see if it's still in one piece! Coming Joan?"

"Yes Richard!" Said Joan. "I'll just go and put our things in our cases first. Perhaps John would give me a hand to carry them home?"

"No problem Mum!" John replied. "I'll go and get mine from Marion's room and I'll be with you!"

Half an hour later John and his parents left to return to their own house.

Pauline, Marion and Sue cleared away the camp beds in the dining room and Marion's bedroom, while David and Julian rearranged the furniture and tidied up before getting the vacuum cleaner out.

Before long their house was looking a lot more like a home.

Tim came down and sat at the table with Pauline to work at some of his school exercises.

"That looks better!" Said Sue. "With luck we can resume our normal lives again now!"

"We will have to go home tomorrow!" Said Julian. "I've got to get back to work and Tim is looking forward to getting back to his School!"

"Yes!" Said Marion. "And Pauline needs to start her anti-natal classes to get ready for their new arrival!"

"And we have a wedding to plan!" Said David with a grin. "Unless the two main players have changed their minds!"

"Well this one hasn't Dad!" Said Marion quickly. "You won't get out of the wedding planning that easy!"

"I don't think John's likely to change his mind either David!" Said Sue.

At that moment they heard the doorbell ring.

"Who can that be?" Said Sue.

"The only way to find out is to open the door Sue!" Said David with a grin.

Sue glared at him, but got up and went to the front door.

When she opened it she saw Bulldog standing there.

"Is John still here?" Asked Bulldog. "I heard a rumour that Vincent Sutherford had been found up in Manchester! Is it true?"

"Yes its true! Good news travels fast!"Said Sue quickly. "John has just gone home with his parents, but come in and we'll tell you what's happened!"

Marion came to the door when she heard Bulldogs voice.

"Come and sit down Bulldog!" She said taking him into the lounge. "It's good to be free from worry of Vincent taking pot shots at us! Isn't It?"

Sue filled in the details of Vincent's confession for Bulldog's benefit.

"Are you going back to your parents!" Asked Sue. "Now that Vincent has been arrested?"

"No I think I will wait a little while, to hear who the couple were that were killed in the crashes!" Said Bulldog. "It will be good to tie up a few loose ends!"

"As it turned out you were the only one that Vincent hurt!" Said Marion. "Apart from me being kidnapped, of course! But I wasn't injured, you were shot and could have been killed!"

At that moment there was another ring of the doorbell!

Sue answered it and John came into the lounge!

"I thought I saw you coming Bulldog!" Said John. "I take it you heard the news via the grapevine! We're just waiting for the last piece in the jigsaw, as I'm sure Sue or Marion's just told you!"

"Yes John!" Said Bulldog happily. "I was telling them, I am waiting to hear the rest of Vincent's confession before going back to my parents!"

"I'm glad you stayed on Bulldog!" Said John seriously. "Not just because we are waiting to hear what Vincent is going hopefully to reveal! There is another reason as far as I'm concerned!"

"Sorry! I don't follow you!" Said Bulldog looking puzzled.

"It's just that I wanted to ask you to do me a favour!" Said John.

"No problem!" Said Bulldog at once. "What's the problem?"

"There isn't a problem!" Said John with a smile. "I wanted to ask you if you would agree to be my Best Man at my wedding to Marion!"

"Of course I would John!" Said Bulldog once again. "It would be an honour!"

"It's a pity I couldn't have two Best Men, Bulldog!" Said John. "I would like Josh to be at our wedding as well! You have both been good friends to me over the last few difficult months!"

"I'm sure we can find something important for Josh as well!" Said Marion with a grin. "After all it does seem a bit unfair that Brides can have several Bridesmaids while the Bridegroom only gets one Best Man! Doesn't it?"

Sue had listened quietly to the conversation.

"Well I'm glad John chose you Bulldog!" Said Sue happily. "Can I call you Walter now though? Even though I think I will always think of you as Bulldog!"

"Yes!" Laughed Bulldog. "Somehow I don't think my Mum would approve of me calling myself Bulldog when I go home. In fact I still don't know if I will be welcomed home at all, yet!"

"After all that you have been through I can't imagine your Mum would not be pleased to have you back!" Said Sue fervently. "I certainly would!"

"I would add my feelings to that!" Said Marion. "Without your help I would not be sitting here now! And I would not be looking forward to my wedding to John!"

"Enough of this mutual admiration talk!" Said Sue. "I'll leave you to it while I go and make you a pot of tea!"

At that moment Bulldogs mobile phone rang.

"Excuse me!" Said Bulldog as he took out his phone and answered it.

"It's Josh!" Said Bulldog and continued. "Hi Josh! Yes the rumours were correct! Yes the scumbag has been arrested up in Manchester! I'll tell you the details later! Hang on Josh! John wants a word! I'll pass him over! Bye!"

"Hi Josh!" Said John. "Now that the coasts clear! Do you want some more reading and writing practice? You do! OK! How about the day after tomorrow? Right I'll see you then! Same time? OK? I'll pass you back to Bulldog!"

Bulldog spent a few minutes talking to Josh before ringing off!

"Josh's brother is taking his driving test next week!" Said Bulldog. "It's a bit soon but he was offered a cancellation, so he took it! I hope he passes! He's a good guy!"

"Yes! I agree!" Said John. "They're both nice blokes! Let's hope Josh gets a decent job as well!"

Sue came in with a tray of tea cups plus milk sugar and a fresh pot of tea.

She was followed by David and Julian, while Pauline remained in the dining room with Tim!

"Mum and Dad asked me to let them know if we hear any more from the Police!" Said John. "They are giving the house the once over, now that things are getting back to normal!"

"It was interesting to hear that Vincent knew the two people that died!" Said Julian.

"Yes I was thinking the same thing!" Said Bulldog. "I had assumed he knew the man flying the Para-Glider, but I was a bit surprised he knew the woman as well!"

"It does mean that she was not there by accident!" Said John. "So I wonder what her role should have been!"

"Perhaps we will find out, if this Vincent guy agrees to talk!" Said David. "It's amazing how one person can cause so much trouble for so many people, for no real reason!"

"Pauline, Tim and I will be leaving after lunch Dad!" Said Julian. "There is a train about 1 o'clock , so can you drop us off at the Station?"

"Of course Julian!" Replied David. "It's been nice seeing you all, in spite of the turn of events you've had to put up with!"

"I don't think we will hear from the Police until tomorrow!" Said Sue. "When we do I'll let you and Pauline know what happens then, Julian!"

Bulldog thanked Sue for the tea and left to go and see Josh and his brother to explain what was happening with regards to Vincent confession etc.

Marion and Sue sorted out something for a quick lunch for everyone as Julian got his family ready to return home!

After lunch there were a series of hurried goodbyes as David took Julian, Pauline and Tim to the train Station!

Half an hour later there was another knock at the door!

Marion opened it and found there were contractors coming to remove the Police Control room from the lawn in the rear garden!

She took them through to the garden for them to remove the building and repair any damage to the lawn and bedding plots!

John suggested he and Marion went into town while the house and garden were returned to the way they were a couple of days ago! He rang Bulldog and invited him and Josh to join them for a coffee and a bite to eat!

They all arrived in the town centre and Marion led them to a café near the place where John used to work!

Josh brought his brother Nat with him so the five of them sat down and had a pleasant chat about the events that they had all shared!

CHAPTER 17 - Conclusions.

The next day one of the Plain Clothed police detectives called to report that Vincent Sutherford had been re-interviewed by Manchester Police and had completed his confession. He was remanded in the Prison Hospital while he was being assessed by psychiatric staff to decide whether he was fit mentally to stand trial! They were first presented with another copy of his original confession :-

Copy of his initial response :-

He claims his actions were instigated by a pathological hatred of Gareth Westerfield for a variety of reasons. When the object of his hatred disappeared his loathing was transferred towards the person he associated with being the female companion of Gareth. This person he believed had the surname of Morrison. He believed this Morrison female married someone called Ashmore after Gareth disappeared.

He also knew there was a Julian Ashmore at Sheffield at the same time as himself and Gareth. He made inquiries and found there was a Marion Ashmore living at the address which the Ashmore at University was registered at. He therefore assumed that Marion Ashmore was the married name of Marion Morrison, and therefore the former girlfriend of Gareth. When he looked on the electoral roll for this address there was no Julian Ashmore registered here only Marion Ashmore. He then made yet another assumption by believing Marion Ashmore (nee Morrison) was divorced from Julian Ashmore. He arrived outside this address one evening just as Marion was meeting John Taylor. His warped mind imagined John Taylor was a colleague of Gareth and that he was acting as a go between for Marion and Gareth. So he took the opportunity to kidnap Marion, hoping to use her to flush out Gareth. When nothing happened after a couple of days he decided to try and get hold of John Taylor. That's why he tried to lure John to Drakes Mill. This misfired when John turned up with Walter Handley (who John knew as Bulldog). He thought Walter was Gareth and shot him. He thought he had killed him, so he left the scene and rode off on his motor cycle. When he learnt later that it wasn't Gareth that he shot (and he had not killed Walter), he turned his attention back to John again, to try to get him to reveal the whereabouts of Gareth. It is not clear, in his mind, why he decided to try and get John to go up to Devil's Rock , and the events it led to are therefore rather confused. More so because two people died as a result of it.

He has however revealed that he knew both of the people that died, but he has not yet agreed to identify them.

They were then presented with Vincent Sutherford's latest Confession!

This is the latest response received today:-

When I realised that I was mistaken in my conviction that John Taylor was not involved with Gareth Westerfield and Marion Ashmore was not in fact Marion Morrison I knew that I had to move away from the area and return home! I had to find a way to extract myself from going to Devil's Rock. I realised I had intended to go up there and attempt to kill the wrong person! Since I had already attempted to kill the person that I was convinced was Gareth, I did not want to become a murderer! Of course I could merely not have turned up, but I had made up my mind therefore that I needed to get someone else to go up to Devil's Rock in my place! For some reason I convinced myself that I needed time to get away from the area! I had already decided to use a Para-Glider to travel up there, so I needed someone else to take my place on it! I had learnt to Para-Glide up in Yorkshire after I left University and I came down to Essex a year ago to continue with my hobby! I met a Microlight enthusiast called Maurice Edwards at my flying club, who was married, but needing money because he was having an affair with a young woman pilot! I convinced him to steal his own Microlight and his car and trailer in order to claim the insurance money for its loss! He agreed and I helped him to do so one evening! I went with him to collect the Microlight and its trailer using a stolen car instead of his one! We hid the trailer containing the Microlight in a disused Barn over in Kent! He duly claimed the insurance money that was paid out when the trailer was not recovered! Since I knew what had happened I realised I could blackmail him to agree to fly my Para-Glider up to Devil's Rock instead of me! He reluctantly agreed to do so, but I could not persuade him to fire at John! He did however agree to take a gun loaded with blanks! I wanted him to impersonate me of course, so I decided to ensure he did not fly away after flying up there! I needed him to be captured in my place! So I decided to sabotage the Para-Glider to cause him to land it! On the Monday morning I went early to the Glider and weakened the lines to the parachute! I must have done the job too well, because I obviously did not intend to kill the pilot! I also did not know that the man had told his girlfriend what he had agreed to do, so I was surprised to learn that she must have agreed to fly the 'stolen' Microlight to pick him up if he had been forced to land!

I'm truly sorry that I was inadvertently responsible for their deaths! I still do not know the identity of the woman, but no doubt the Police down there will be able to find it now!

Signed Vincent Sutherford.

Marion and John were still sorry for the deaths of the two people, but pleased that their identities had now been established! They felt no sympathy for Vincent however, because of all the trouble that he had caused them both plus the injury to Bulldog!

John rang Bulldog and informed him what they had heard!

CHAPTER 18 - Epilogue

John and Marion's lives now returned to something approaching normality after the last few weeks of uncertainty.

Bulldog finally went back to his family in Nottingham - his family were delighted to receive him back!

Vincent Sutherford was finally declared fit to stand trial and was sentenced to 12 years for his crimes.

The following year John and Marion finally married with Walter (no longer called Bulldog) returning to be best man!

Tosh eventually got a job as an assistant to an local established interior painter and decorator! Nathan, Josh's brother passed his driving test, obtained an HGB license and became a Long Distance Lorry Driver!

THE END

29965060R00099

Printed in Poland
by Amazon Fulfillment
Poland Sp. z o.o., Wrocław